"You are angry—at me?" Cecelia guessed from the duke's expression. Had he really found out about her and Percy? She suddenly recalled his remark about being "concerned about her feelings for Percival." Had he said that as a hint that he knew of them?

"Is it my—relationship with Percival?" she forced herself to ask.

The duke smiled wryly. "I know it should not matter. In fact, I cannot say why it—annoyed me so much for you to say you loved the man."

"I—"

Julian looked down at the confusion in the lovely eyes meeting his so anxiously, and his own gaze softened. "No, that was not the truth," he admitted, raising one hand to gently stroke down her cheek. "I was not just annoyed. I was—jealous because you were speaking of Levison—instead of me."

"Your Grace—?" Cecelia's eyes were filled with wonder at something sweet and warm that seemed to bloom within her at his touch—his words.

The duke drew in his breath at the look in her eyes, forgetting all but an aching need. "My name is Julian, my love," he corrected, his lips lowering to hers.

"Julian." Forgetting who the duke thought she was, Cecelia murmured his name against his lips, her arms sliding about the duke's neck quite naturally as he drew her to him . . .

WATCH FOR THESE ZEBRA REGENCIES

LADY STEPHANIE   (0-8217-5341-X, $4.50)
by Jeanne Savery
Lady Stephanie Morris has only one true love: the family estate she has
managed ever since her mother died. But then Lord Anthony Rider
arrives on her estate, claiming he has plans for both the land and the
woman. Stephanie soon realizes she's fallen in love with a man whose
sensual caresses will plunge her into a world of peril and intrigue . . .
a man as dangerous as he is irresistible.

BRIGHTON BEAUTY   (0-8217-5340-1, $4.50)
by Marilyn Clay
Chelsea Grant, pretty and poor, naively takes school friend Alayna
Marchmont's place and spends a month in the country. The devastating
man had sailed from Honduras to claim his promised bride, Miss
Marchmont. An affair of the heart may lead to disaster . . . unless a
resourceful Brighton beauty finds a way to stop a masquerade and keep
a lord's love.

LORD DIABLO'S DEMISE   (0-8217-5338-X, $4.50)
by Meg-Lynn Roberts
The sinfully handsome Lord Harry Glendower was a gambler and the
black sheep of his family. About to be forced into a marriage of con-
venience, the devilish fellow engineered his own demise, never having
dreamed that faking his death would lead him to the heavenly refuge
of spirited heiress Gwyn Morgan, the daughter of a physician.

A PERILOUS ATTRACTION   (0-8217-5339-8, $4.50)
by Dawn Aldridge Poore
Alissa Morgan is stunned when a frantic passenger thrusts her baby into
Alissa's arms and flees, having heard rumors that a notorious highwayman posed a threat to their coach. Handsome stranger Hugh Sebastian
secretly possesses the treasured necklace the highwayman seeks and
volunteers to pose as Alissa's husband to save her reputation. With a
lost baby and missing necklace in their care, the couple embarks on a
journey into peril—and passion.

*Available wherever paperbacks are sold, or order direct from the
Publisher. Send cover price plus 50¢ per copy for mailing and
handling to Penguin USA, P.O. Box 999, c/o Dept. 17109, Ber-
genfield, NJ 07621. Residents of New York and Tennessee must
include sales tax. DO NOT SEND CASH.*

LADY CECELIA'S CHARADE

Jacquelyn Gillis

Zebra Books
Kensington Publishing Corp.

http://www.zebrabooks.com

ZEBRA BOOKS are published by

Kensington Publishing Corp.
850 Third Avenue
New York, NY 10022

First Printing: December, 1996

Printed in the United States of America

10   9   8   7   6   5   4   3   2   1

Chapter One

"You, go on *stage!* Sissy, have you lost your wits?" Percival Levison stopped his anxious pacing across the elegant parquet floor of his cousin's parlor to stare at her in shock.

The young lady's lips tightened stubbornly. "Percy, listen. We both know your plays are excellent. All you have needed was a chance to present them and now with this Duke of Standish willing to—"

"Stanford."

"What?" Cecelia frowned at having her enthusiastic train of thought interrupted.

"He's the Duke of Stanford," Percival clarified patiently.

Cecelia sighed. "Oh, Standish—Stanford—I don't care *which* duke he is. With any duke willing to have his theater produce *Justine*—"

"Well, he's not exactly having his theater produce it," her cousin again interrupted consideringly. "That is, Barcelly Play House is Stanford's property, of course, but it is not as though the duke has anything to do with the plays, or any such. He merely allows different thespian groups to lease the property for their productions.''

Lady Cecelia Somersett rolled her eyes. "Percival, *must* you always be so precise?''

"I am merely avoiding the possibility of embarrassing error," he said with a repressive glance. "After all, one can only imagine how aghast the ton would be on the suggestion that one of their prime members was in trade.''

Cecelia raised her brows expressively. "Heaven forbid! Did I suggest that? A nobleman stooping to—actually *earning* his living—rather than frittering his inheritance away in the gambling halls?''

"Now Sissy," Percival grinned at his cousin's exaggerated tone, "don't go climbing on that high horse again. If I could ever get you to post down to London, you would discover all 'lords' are not like that viscount, you developed a *tendre* for—''

"—at sixteen!" Cecelia snapped with a foreboding glare at her younger cousin. "When I was yet too green to know better. But Richard was not the only such 'lord' nosing about my meager inheritance, or perhaps you've forgotten the Earl of Kressing—whose offer of marriage included settling his gambling debts? Or Lord Whiffers, so into dun territory with the cents-per-cents that he had to flee the country and missed our spring ball after exacting an invitation from *you* to get to meet me, or— let me think, I believe the next was Lord Alvers, the baron who spends more on his hunters—''

"All right, I suppose I can concede that you have run into a coxcomb or two." Percival shrugged. "But that is to be expected. You are highly eligible, as a baroness in your own right with an estate the size of Somersett.

One must expect that to give hope to some—less desirable suitors.''

"Must one expect such?'' Cecelia sniffed. "And all these 'suitors' flocking to the highly 'eligible' Baroness of—what? An enormous debt ridden estate, that I'm not allowed to sell an acre of land even to feed the cattle because it's entailed to some great-grandchild I'll probably never have! What fustian! I wish our grandmothers had been switched. I don't care anything about the title. You would fit so much better into the ton than I, Percy.''

The slight young man shuddered at the thought. "Heavens! I'm quite pleased with my status, thank you. And you are doing marvelously keeping Somersett from the gullgropers. I fear I should never have time to write my plays, were I 'lord of the manor' trying to keep this place going. Nor can I image Constance giving routs and musicales or sitting about exchanging *on-dits* with other young matrons during morning calls.''

Cecelia laughed, typically back in good humor. "Nor can I! Constance would be instantly labeled a bluestocking. How is she doing anyway? She must be close to birthing, is she not? Are you quite certain I should not go up to Berwick to be with her? It is only a day's journey.''

Percival blushed at his cousin's casual reference to his wife's condition. "She would love to see you I am sure, but there is really no need, as her mother is with her.''

"Oh yes, you are staying at Hampton Manor still—''

"I thought perhaps you had forgotten the last time you visited us.'' Percival observed in amusement. "If I recall correctly, Constance's four younger brothers had you ready for bedlam before tea?''

"They were just being boys, of course, but as you say,

Constance does have her mother and I should probably
be in the way—"

Percival did not even bother denying the excuse as
Cecelia quickly resumed their previous topic. "That
reminds me, you intend using the proceeds from your
play to obtain your own residence, do you not?"

"Yes, which is but one of the reasons I am so anxious
to have this play succeed." Percival sighed. "Though I
adore Constance's family, it does get a bit trying with
so many in one household."

"Percy, I have told you, you are more than welcome
to live here at Somersett. Heaven only knows, I rattle
about in this monstrosity by myself." Cecelia reiterated
the oft issued invitation. "After all, both of our families
lived here when we were children and we rubbed along
quiet well."

"I do appreciate the offer, Sissy," her cousin smiled,
absently taking a seat before the fire, though his cousin
yet stood. "But, as you know, I never dealt well with the
sea air here, even when a child. Not to mention that I
doubtless should never get Constance to move so far
from her own home," he added, placing another log
onto the andirons as the summer rains had cooled the
morning considerably.

Encouraged that Percival had settled down enough
to relax, Cecelia joined him on the settee. "I can scarcely
blame Constance, wanting to be near her family. And,
now that you mention it, I recall you did seem inclined
to put out a rash whenever we played at the Firth," she
added mischievously.

"It was something about the salt air." Percival grimaced. "I shall never forget those many nights spent
coated with Nanny Blake's foul smelling unguent."

Cecelia chuckled, moving deftly back to her plan.
"Well, truly, there is no reason why with proceeds from

your plays you should not be able to support your own household. All you need is a chance to present one of your plays before a proper audience. Your writing is much too sophisticated for the country villagers who attend performances by those traveling troupes.''

"I know, but up until now, they were my *only* audience. It was one of those performances though, that brought me to Stanford's attention. He spotted *Justine* playing at a fair near his country seat and was quite enthusiastic about its potential. Without even my asking, he offered up the use of his theater *and* said he would provide financial backing.''

"This duke obviously has good taste, at least." Cecelia nodded. "Though I imagine his generosity was based on the confidence that he would receive a good return for his investment.''

"Yes, the return on his investment!" Percival's countenance tightened. "That is my main concern, above even my own profit. Stanford has put an alarming amount of blunt into producing this play, Sissy. More even than I would ever have asked. He insisted on everything being of the first stare—costumes, props, music—" He paused, sighing. "It was going to be a magnificent production—and then that accursed Miriam runs off with some bogus count from the continent! And on this short of notice, I can not image how I shall find a replacement for the female lead.''

Cecelia stood in exasperation. "Percy, that is what I am trying to tell you. That is no problem. I am quite sure I can—"

"No." Percival stopped her firmly. "The idea of your playing Justine is totally out of the question. I would have never stopped by here on my way back to London, if I had dreamed you would come up with such a harebrained notion! I merely thought you might know of someone for the part. You take an interest in the village choir. You have not come across any local singers who might take the part?"

"No. At least not anyone I should allow to ruin that lovely play of yours. But do listen—"

"No, Cecelia. Please—you are *not* playing Justine!" Percival Levison shook his head in amazement at his scatter-brained relative. Though his favorite cousin was two years his senior, it seemed it always fell on him to try to counsel her out of some rackety behavior or the other. Not that he often managed to change her mind. In fact, Percival suddenly recalled in some alarm, all too many times she had managed to talk him into joining her!

"Percy, just listen to me a minute." Cecelia excitedly rose from the damask settee, determined not to give up on this adventure her young cousin had unwittingly offered her. "You know I played the role of Countess Evangeline in your production last Christmas. All of our relatives said I did remarkably well. Why, even you joked on how I had surely 'missed my calling.' "

"Cecelia, that was a Christmas play at our great-aunt Honoria's home. That is not at all like going on a London stage in front of strangers. It is simply not done! I do not mean to offend your sensibilities, my dear, but only females of—well"—he stammered in embarrassment—"*questionable* character present themselves on a public stage."

"Percy, you are such a dear," Cecelia giggled. "Please recall that I am two-and-twenty years of age. I know about women of questionable character, and the like. Of course, I could not appear as myself! I will find some disguise—" she mused, expanding on the possibilities. "No one in society really knows actresses anyway. Justine can be from somewhere else—maybe an unfortunate émigré from France you came upon in Northern England? That will bring even more attention to your play, do you not think?''

"No! Sissy, there is absolutely *no way* I would ever allow you to do such a thing!'' Percival stood with a sudden sense of urgency to be out of his cousin's influence. "Now, I am sorry, but I really must be going if I am to get back in London by the morrow.''

Cecelia sighed in frustration as she sought to come up with some means of persuasion. Percival was such a love—he deserved this chance. She could do it, she knew she could! And what fun it would be! It had been ages since anything so interesting had come across her path.

Cecelia had read *Justine* through several times during its writing, so it would take little to memorize her lines and she had no qualms on being able to sing the leading lady's part in the little opera. It was without conceit that Cecelia recognized that she was blessed with an exceptional soprano voice.

Her voice? Maybe? Cecelia paused at the sudden thought. As tender hearted as Percival was, he would not be able to bear thinking he had hurt her feelings. The young lady did hesitate a moment at the devious nature of the plan, but then easily rationalized that concern away. After all, it was for her cousin's own good.

Carefully lowering her tone to one of soulful acceptance, Cecelia stopped her cousin as he prepared to leave. "Forgive me, Percival. It was quite ill of me to pressure you. I just—was not thinking. Of course, you would want someone with a voice—worthy of your play.''

"I am glad you have regained some sense of—'' Percival began in relief before her words sank in. "What do you mean worthy? This has nothing to do with your abilities."

"Pray do not dissemble, cousin, it is quite all right." Cecelia's smile was brave, though she pointedly drew a lace handkerchief from her sleeve. "I know my voice is untrained, and certainly not up to singing professional opera."

"Untrained?" Percival looked at her perplexed. "Cecelia, you have the most lovely soprano voice I have ever heard. That has nothing at all to do with allowing you to expose yourself on a public stage—"

"Oh." She looked away to hide her delight at this new weapon her cousin most conveniently offered. "I see. I understand that at my age, I am no longer in the first blush of beauty, but I thought—" As the handkerchief was raised, Percival hurried to Cecelia's side.

"Sissy, Sissy, I did not mean to imply anything against your looks, my dear!" the innocent young man cried in horror. "Why you are absolutely lovely. Surely you know that? There is not a lady in London to hold a candle to you. Oh heavens, my dear, you shain't cry?"

"Cry?" At that moment Hannah, Cecelia's young abigail, came into the parlor and looked at her mistress in disbelief. Cecelia never cried about anything.

The lady in question managed to give her maid a warning look from around the bit of lace.

"Oh." Hannah stopped a smile. "Oh my, Mr. Levison, what have you said to upset Miss Cecelia?" She glared at the young man, wondering just what her unpredictable mistress was up to this time.

"I did not mean to upset her—that is. Oh, please Hannah, tell Cecelia she has no need for concern on her beauty. Why my love, you are still quite as beautiful as ever."

"Still!" Cecelia gasped in faked dismay.

"No-no, that is not what I meant at all." Percival was becoming frantic.

"You mean—I am *not* still as beautiful?" Cecelia moaned in an even more tremulous tone.

"Yes, of course you are. I just meant not—still—" At his cousin's sob, Percival desperately turned to the abigail. "Hannah!"

"I believe I should go fetch a tea tray," Hannah murmured, deciding it best to be uninvolved when her mistress was doubtless about to get young Percival to do something dreadfully untoward.

"We are going to London?" Hannah stared at her mistress in surprise, later that morning. "But I thought you despised the ton?"

"Yes, that is true. It is such a crush. But we, dear Hannah, are not going to be exactly—in the ton. In fact, we shall be quite outside the pale of society entirely," Cecelia advised, crossing her bedroom to a grand mahogany wardrobe.

"Oh dear, Miss Cecelia. Now this ain't liable to land us in Newgate like your last caper almost did?" The abigail looked at her anxiously.

"Hannah, Hannah." Cecelia pulled out a long unused dinner gown from the wardrobe, and held it up for inspection. "Those Bow Streeters never even got close to us. And it is not as though we harmed anyone. Why, I was extremely careful in prying open that crate so as not to cause damage." She held the gown up to her. "Is this watered silk too sadly out of date, do you suppose?"

"What we did, was illegal, miss." Her lips pursed, Hannah ignored the attempted change of topic.

"Well, the posting house should have allowed the

public to view that mummy when it came through anyway.'' Cecelia was unrepentant. "After all, it was going on display in London. Imagine, expecting us to make a two-day trip when it passed right through here! If I had not taken matters in hand, we might never have seen it.''

Hannah shuddered. "I shouldn't have minded missing it myself. You did not tell me we were going to see a dried-up dead body!''

"Well," Cecelia gave her maid a guilty glance, "I suppose I did just rather assume you knew what a mummy was. But you must admit, it was quite exciting.''

"It was that, fair enough." The abigail gave up with a chuckle, cocking her head to study the evening dress critically. "However, from now on, miss, I prefer my excitement to be at least *legal.*''

"Well, there is certainly nothing illegal about this—" Cecelia managed convincingly, though not at all sure. "However, it perhaps is not overly—proper.''

"Not *proper?*" Hannah turned back to her mistress in alarm. "Now, Miss Cecelia, you would not—''

"Silly goose," Cecelia interrupted, laughing, "I was just teasing you. Of course I would never do anything really improper—well, at least, not *too* improper," she mitigated at the abigail's disbelieving look. "I merely intend helping Percival with his plays. This Duke of Stanford has been backing the production of *Justine* but now suddenly Percy's leading lady has abandoned him, so—''

Cecelia's abigail was more difficult to convince than her cousin, but the young lady's persuasiveness, coupled with the treat of a month in London, eventually brought Hannah around.

* * *

"Mr. Percival will be able to supply us with the theatrical make-up for your disguise, miss. And, look what I have here." Hannah triumphantly displayed a small corked bottle, the following day.

"What is it?" Cecelia folded her favorite paisley shawl into the trunk Hannah had left open.

"It is henna." The abigail grinned.

"Henna? What is that?" Cecelia took the bottle curiously.

"A potion used to color hair."

"What? You are suggesting I *dye* my hair!" Cecelia exclaimed, startled at the notion even more daring than any of her own.

"Yes. It is all right. Claudette down at the Red Rooster gave that to me. Of course, I didn't tell her who it was for." Hannah quickly assuaged Cecelia's aghast look. "You did say you wanted to be disguised and what better way than to change your coloring? I cannot imagine anyone would ever connect a fiery-haired Justine with the elegant, blond Lady Somersett?"

"Oh Hannah, I could never—I mean—you are saying this would turn my hair—*red?*" Cecelia stared at the little bottle in dismay.

The abigail laughed. "Of course, it's not permanent. I wouldn't think of doing anything to harm that lovely hair of yours. This is just a temporary color. Claudette assured me you would be able to wash it right out, whenever you wish."

"Oh, it washes out—" Cecelia considered a moment, before grinning, "I believe you are right, Hannah, auburn tresses would suit Justine much better than my own blond hair."

Chapter Two

Even Cecelia was not bold enough to risk staying at her own house off Regent's Park while acting in the play, so Percival had leased them other accommodations.

"I am sorry Sissy, but you know my finances," Percival apologized at his cousin's poorly disguised dismay as he delivered them to an unprepossessing terrace house several days later.

"I wish I could have provided better but I am afraid this is all I can afford with my current state of finances." Percival didn't mention that even these lodgings were let utilizing the duke's advanced funds.

Stanford had, of course, given him permission to charge necessary items for the production on his accounts, and surely, Percival reasoned, a leading lady was the most important item of all.

"Don't concern yourself, Percy. This shall suffice fine." Cecelia forced a bright smile, nudging her scowling abigail to silence. "After all, it is only for a short while and I'm certain it's pleasant enough inside."

"Well," her cousin hedged, nervously opening the door, "it does need a bit of cleaning, but I have got a domestic service sending out staff immediately."

"Hm, it appears to have been—closed for awhile." Cecelia coughed discreetly on entering the dank, musty smelling building.

Hannah's haughty sniff was not near so tactful. "Miss, surely you don't intend us staying in this—"

"We shall manage quite well, Hannah," Cecelia interceded quickly. "All these apartments need is a bit of cleaning—and uh—decorating. You—did say you have hired the staff already, Percy?" She had not dared bring any of the other Somersett staff, who though quite loyal, might have somehow let her identity slip out.

"Yes. Well, not *hired* exactly—that is, I did not have time to interview anyone as yet, but the agency is sending them out for approval." Percival busily moved from the entry on into the small octagonal parlour. "I say, this room is rather pleasant, is it not?"

Cecelia didn't miss her cousin's sudden change of topic. "What agency? Was it Berkham's? They have always supplied our extra town staff."

"Berkham's? Well, no, it was a uh, smaller agency." Percival hedged not wishing to elaborate on Smythe's Domestics, an establishment chosen entirely for its low fee.

To his relief, before Cecelia could question him further, the clattering of wheels came from outside. "Ah, perhaps that is the servants arriving now." Percival hopefully crossed to the window and pushed aside the heavy velvet drapes. "Excellent, the hackney is stopping. I am sure the servants will have this place spotless in no time." He dropped the drape back into place and great eddies of dust wafted from its folds.

Cecelia stepped back from the window, coughing.

"Of course they will. Uh, why don't we go outside and greet them?" she suggested.

Although it was scarcely correct protocol to meet one's servants on the steps, neither argued.

"I certainly hope this agency sent some decent people," Hannah muttered darkly as the hackney steadied his horses.

"I told the proprietor to only send the very best he had," Percival assured them, not mentioning that he had said the best, for the lowest salary.

"Well, then, I am sure—" Cecelia began but her words dwindled to disbelieving silence as a positively ancient man in faded butler's attire sidled down the hackney steps.

"Careful now, lovey, them steps is a mite high," a florid-faced woman, as rotund as the man was thin, hung onto his arm to steady him. "There now." The carriage springs protested as she heaved her own mass down the thin metal steps. "Let's hope these here folks is—" finally glancing up, the woman saw the three people standing before the house. "Oh, lordy—Wally, they's already here awaitin' us. Hurry on up."

She rushed ahead of the aged man, to bob nervous curtsies to the astonished trio with no discernment on their varying statuses.

"Milord, miladies, I be Martha Cochran sent out from Miz Smythe's agency as y'er cook and this here is Mr. Wordsworth, y'er butler." She gave an anxious gesture of encouragement to the old man. "Come on along, Wally. We be 'ere to serve you." She bobbed yet again before turning back to the hackney.

"Eh! Bring those boxes on up 'ere, boy!"

The woman's shrill order seemed to startle Cecelia and Percival into action.

"Um, wait—" Cecelia began just as Percival waved back the coachman.

"Just a moment, coachman." Avoiding Cecelia's eyes, Percival cleared his throat. "Uh, actually, Mrs.—Cochran, the agency was to send persons out to be—interviewed for the positions, and we—I have not yet made any firm decision—so I should not think you would wish to have the fellow unload your trunks—" He stopped as the woman made a vague choking sound.

"Oh, no! Please, milord. You ain't go' say we can't 'ave the post? That woman at Smythe's said if we get sent back a'gin she's plumb taking us off the list for good! Misses?" Her eyes leaped imploringly between the two women. "I'm a 'ard worker, I am. And Wal—uh, Mr. Wordsworth 'ere ain't always so slow. 'E's just tired, you see. He 'adn't 'ad much sleep as we cleaned all night on that Smythe's Service place. But Wally, he's a fine butler—"

"Uh, Mrs. Cochran—" Percival tried to interrupt but she kept right on.

" 'E's worked for nobles all 'is born days."

"It's all right, Martha. I told you it wasn't any use," the old man sighed, finally hobbling up beside her. "No one wants the likes of us anymore."

"Now you 'ush up, Wally. 'Course they do." The woman gently brushed at a slightly dustier spot on the man's threadbare black cutaway. "Milord, you ain't got to worry about paying us that five shillings like Miz Smythe said. Why, three will be aplenty—or two even, what with somewheres to sleep and a crust o' bread or two and—"

"I'm really sorry, Mrs. Cochran." Percival finally managed in a reasonably firm voice, but stopped in dismay as the cook's lower lip trembled and two big tears rolled down her cheek. He turned in near panic to Cecelia.

"Sissy—"

His cousin sighed. "What Mr. Levison means is, he's agreed to five shilling and five it shall be. Now Percy, perhaps you would advise the coachman to bring these good people's belongings in?"

Hannah rolled her eyes as Cecelia took the old man's elbow to help him up the steps. "Here Mr. Wordsworth. Now do be careful, that second step seems a bit loose."

"Bless you, miss!" Martha hurried along behind. "You ain't go' be sorry, miss. Wally, 'e'll fix that there step for you, milady. Won't you Wally? Jes' soon as 'e rests up a bit. And, lord love us, just look at all this dust!" she exclaimed at the small entry hall. "Well, don't you go frettin' none, milady. I'll 'ave it all just neater-'n-a-pin in no time. I'll just start right now—"

Cecelia stopped her as she pulled a ragged plaid kerchief from some pocket of the worn, voluminous skirt and began earnestly rubbing at the nearest table. "There is plenty of time for that later, Mrs. Cochran. Why don't you and Wordsworth settle yourselves in your rooms first. Hannah, would you be so kind as to show them the way?"

"Yes, of course," replied Hannah with a look her mistress wisely pretended not to see.

"Oh," Cecelia recalled, "is the maid coming later?"

"Maid?" The two servants looked at one another. "Miz Smythe said the gentleman only paid for the two of us, but I can cook and 'andle this 'ere place fine. You won't be needing no maid."

Cecelia smiled carefully. "Well, you may go on to your rooms. I must have a brief word with Mr. Levison before he leaves."

* * *

"Now, Sissy, you knew I couldn't afford anything like you are accustomed to at Somersett. Two servants were all I could manage." Percival glanced longingly toward his own carriage as the hackney vanished down the street.

Cecelia sighed in defeat. "I know. We certainly do not live in a grand manner at Somersett these days either. I wish I had the funds to help you myself but I have been as pinch pursed as you, trying to support that mausoleum of a property."

"Cecelia, I would *never* have asked you for money!" Her cousin's face turned scarlet. "And, I shall of course, pay you your full share of everything the play earns," he added huffily.

Cecelia realized in chagrin that she had insulted her young relative, in even implying that he might have borrowed from her. "Well sir, I should certainly *hope* you intend paying me!" she sniffed pretentiously. "As I believe that is customary with one's *femme de joille?*"

As expected, Percival forgot his hurt dignity. "Cecelia!" he gasped, glancing about in alarm least anyone had heard.

His cousin giggled. "What, Percy? That was our decision—that I should pose as your—ahem, mistress, so I should not be open to unwelcome advances from other males, was it not?"

"Yes—no! Oh, I do not know!" The young man ran his hand distractedly through his habitually disarrayed sandy hair. "That was all your idea back at Somersett! I cannot imagine how I let you convince me that such an arrangement was in any manner reasonable," he groaned. "But I am truly sorry. I—I do not think I can manage this any further. No, this just is not going to work—"

"Of course it will." Not at all concerned on his vacillating, Cecelia soothingly straightened Percival's coat lapels. "Now you shall see, your play will be an enormous success and then you need not worry a pinch about me. Why, Amber shall star in your play and then vanish immediately back into the mysterious realms from whence she came, Lady Somersett shall reemerge and no one will ever be the wiser."

"I just do not know," Percival repeated distractedly. "I wish I could think of some other alternative, but Stanford has already been more than patient with the blunt he's put into this play and—" All of his cousin's words finally sank in and Percival looked up puzzled. "Amber? Who is Amber?"

"Me." Cecelia grinned. "I decided that shall be my stage name. Amber, rather interestingly French. What do you think?"

"Oh, good heavens," her cousin moaned.

"Now remember the play has only some three weeks until this season's end. By then this duke will see how good you really are and shall doubtless be pleased to continue backing you."

"Three weeks?" Percival hopefully focused on the short period. "I suppose that is not very long. And, who knows, I might even find a replacement for you before then."

"Of course, you might," Cecelia encouraged, "and next season, with Amber but a marquee memory, the reclusive Lady Cecelia Somersett shall open her London house particularly to attend her renowned cousin's plays."

Percival dreamily considered that happy future. "Oh Sissy, you don't know what that would mean to me."

"But back to the immediate necessities," Cecelia said. "I really do fear we shall need a bit more help at least initially putting this house in order."

"I could get Beth, the maid who does my rooms to come over for today if that would help?" Percival offered.

"Yes, that should do fine. Send her now though, and perhaps have her stop at the market on the way, for supper provisions."

Anxious to be away, Percival agreed. "Of course, Sissy. I will go by my rooms on the way to the theater and send her back in a hackney."

"Send her back in *your* carriage, Percy."

"*My* carriage? But Sissy—"

"I shall have need of it as I, doubtless, will have to raid my house in town for decent linens and the like. After all, it was you who insisted I did not dare risk bringing my own coach and I refuse to be going about in a rattler."

The young man's face fell. "Very well. I suppose I can take the hackney—"

"Besides," Cecelia could not resist another jibe, "I believe as you are my protector it is quite expected I should be riding about in your coach, anyway, is it not?"

Percival gave a painful grimace. "I still am not sure we should be doing this, Cecelia. I would not be upset at all if you wish change your mind," he added hopefully.

"I would not think of it." She laughed. "Why, dear cousin, I am quite looking forward to the morrow."

Though coarse, Martha Cochran proved to be worth her considerable weight in gold. In scarcely any time after the other maid arrived, she and Beth had the small accommodations sparkling clean.

Cecelia had left them to their work under Hannah's direction while she and Percival's coachman sojourned to the Somersett town house, to return some hours later with the carriage loaded.

"Why these are beautiful," Martha declared at the various curtains, cushions, linens and bric-a-brac they unloaded. "Where ever did you get it all, Miss Amber?"

Cecelia hesitated a moment before recognizing the name she had given the woman. "Oh, uh, it's just some odd and ends from a relative's place I borrowed," she supplied vaguely. "I found some things that might be of use to you and Mr. Wordsworth as well."

Cecelia brought out a butler's livery purloined from the closets of Somersett. "It may be a bit large but I expect with some minor alteration, it should serve."

Martha took the formal black suit in awe. "Oh miss! Wally'll be so very proud. 'E ain't 'ad no proper butler coat in years. And I can fix it right up for 'im in no time, don't you worry none."

Cecelia reached back into the box and pulled out two rather plain but good quality bombazine gowns, the only clothing of large enough size she'd found for the cook. "These were in one of the upstairs trunks. Heaven only knows who they belonged to, but I thought perhaps . . ."

"For me?" The woman's eyes glowed. "I can sure use them. Why they won't require 'ardly any lettin' out." She happily held one up for effect. "I'll go fix these right now miss, so we'll look all proper when Mr. Levison gets back."

Even Hannah smiled as the woman bustled out. "Well, Miss Amber, I wouldn't have thought it, but this odd arrangement just might work out, though I fear your blessed mother would turn over in her grave if she knew her daughter was going on stage."

"Now Hannah, we've been through all of that before. No one shall have reason to imagine Baroness Somersett even knows of this actress Amber. Which reminds me toward that end, hadn't we best be doing something with this?" She removed the carriage hat that had been covering her thick honey blonde hair since they'd arrived.

Some hours later an altogether different woman hesitantly approached the long peer glass of her bedroom.

"Oh my!" Cecelia surveyed her reflected image in shock. Hannah had styled Cecelia's hair, normally quite straight and silky, into a profusion of auburn curls clustered gaily about her face. The paint pots supplied by Percival had been expertly used. Rouge and eye kohl, that no decent woman admitted to using, had subtly changed Cecelia's features from patrician to provocative. The gown also supplied by Percival, though not truly indiscreet, managed to cling just so, to assure a gentleman's eyes were carefully directed.

"Oh my, my," Cecelia repeated. "I do look like— like some light-skirt!"

"Hm." Hannah considered her, unconcerned. "A little perhaps. But oddly still—ladylike."

"How consoling." Cecelia gave her a wry look. "At least I look like a lady lightskirt."

Percival Levison, even knowing his cousin's abilities, was amazed at the changes on entering the house the next morning.

"Mr. Levison." The old butler, bathed, shaved and properly suited, staidly took the playwright's hat and tiered cape. "Miss Amber awaits you, sir."

"Miss—? Oh yes, Miss Amber." Percival acknowledged weakly as he followed the butler to the small parlor.

"Mr. Levison," the butler announced before bowing out.

Percival came to a dead stop as the woman turned from the mantel toward him. "Good—God!"

"Mister Percival!" the abigail chastised.

Percival ignored Hannah. "Cecelia?" he stared, not quite able to equate his coolly elegant cousin of yesterday with this ravishing creature that stood before him.

"Cecelia?" Cecelia raised an eloquent brow. *"Au contraire, monsieur,* I am Amber—or Justine, *s'il vous plait."*

A smile slowly relaxed the young man's startled features. "Sissy, you are a wonder! I should have known you could do it! No one would ever dream this Amber was Lady Somersett."

Cecelia's confidence however began to ebb later that afternoon as their carriage entered a street of large houses, on their way to the theater.

"This is a lovely area," Cecelia commented in surprise as they turned onto a landscaped drive to Barcelly Play House. "I cannot imagine how a theater, regardless how nice, came to be in such a neighborhood?"

"It is rather impressive, isn't it? In fact, the duke's house itself is on Pall Mall, just beyond the park there." Percival pointed. "Stanford told me his great grandfather, the fifth duke, loved the theater so much that he had Barcelly erected here on his own property for private productions. And after that duke died, the theater continued to be leased out over the next generations. I was quite fortunate that it was available when Stanford approached me."

"It is lovely, but not very large?" Cecelia noted in some concern as the coachman drew Percival's carriage to a halt beside the elegant building.

"Barcelly has a very loyal following in the upper nobility, particularly the duke's friends. So, though it is small, Stanford said we may expect to play to a full house nightly. That is, if the play goes well," he added rather nervously.

Cecelia glanced at her cousin, to find his brow again furrowed in worry. "Of course it shall go well!" she jested to lighten his concern, "It's a lovely play and now, with Amber as your lead, how could it not?"

Percival's smile was only halfhearted as he handed her down from the carriage. "I guess I am a little anxious, but when Stanford extended my credit again last week he made it very plain that it was the last time. This play has *got* to open next Friday—or not at all!"

"Well, if it must open next Friday, then so it shall." Cecelia decried. "After all, *mon cheri,*" she again assumed the seductive French accent. "Have I not told you, your Amber will make everything right? We shall have *beaucoup de richesse, oui?*"

Percival couldn't help laughing. *"Oui!"* He grabbed his cousin and swung her around happily. "Ah, love, with you here, I am beginning to think this just might work after all!"

Neither Percival nor Cecelia had noticed the fine phaeton drawn up under the shade of a huge oak behind them, or its occupant who had been watching the tableau with an inscrutable expression.

"Mr. Levison, I would assume this is the mysterious actress you have told me about?" The duke determined it was time to make his presence known before the two embarrassed themselves further.

"Stanford!" the young playwright gasped, quickly extricating himself from Cecelia's arms as the tall man stepped from the shadows.

"Uh, yes, Your Grace," Percival finally managed.

"May I present my—that is, our new leading lady, Miss uh,—" he glanced at Cecelia in panic.

"Amber," Cecelia supplied coolly, ignoring the duke's raised brow.

"Miss—Amber, you say? Is Amber your surname— or your given?" The chit was absolutely ravishing, Julian realized in surprise. Where in the blue blazes had Levison found her?

"Both," Cecelia decided calmly much to Percival's discomfort.

"Well then, welcome, Amber."

Cecelia felt a strange warmth curl within her at the handsome duke's slow smile.

"I shall look forward to your performance at Barcelly."

"Thank you, Your Grace."

Anxious to be away, Percival took Cecelia's hand pointedly and tucked it about his arm. "I brought Amber down to meet the cast, and begin her rehearsals, as we have not very long to prepare."

"Excellent. You will be rehearsing today?" Stanford commented blandly, rather amused at the playwright's weak attempt to be rid of him. "Perhaps you would not mind if I watch for awhile? I am quite eager to see our new leading lady on the stage."

"And uh, so you shall, Your Grace," Percival said. "But as this is the initial rehearsal with Amber, perhaps, it would be better—that is, you would enjoy it more, some other time?"

Catching the anxious glance that passed between the two, the duke's eyes narrowed in concern. He had assumed the playwright was just being possessive of his ladybird—but that look suggested the matter might be more serious. Why should they mind him watching?

Surely the young pup would not be trying to bring in a ringer on him?

Nothing of the duke's thoughts showed as he placed a friendly hand on the playwright's shoulder, directing them on to the theatre. "Come, my good man, I understand it is a first rehearsal for Amber. And you, my dear," he smiled warmly down at her, "must not be nervous. You do not truly mind if I watch, do you?"

Hardly able to refuse, Cecelia managed a fairly convincing answer.

The small group of people lounging about the stage, came quickly to order as they approached.

"Look, it's our new leading lady!" someone called out and Cecelia was immediately surrounded.

"I'm Daniel. Robert, in the play. So glad to have you with us, love," the male lead, a handsome young Londoner greeted her enthusiastically. "You are Amber, I believe Levison said?"

"Yes."

"Hello, Amber, I'm Vivian, Justine's abigail, Sophia." A petite young woman pushed Daniel aside, playfully. "We're very relieved Mr. Levison found you. We feared the play might not open."

"Thank you, I am quite glad to—"

"And I'm Terrance." Yet another cast member interrupted. "Amber? French, isn't it? I think I saw you in Paris in one of those Dubroi Operas—"

"No, I have not actually—"

Cecelia managed to muddle through the introductions and interested questions, all too aware of the duke casually leaning at the stage entrance listening.

Percival finally came to her rescue. "All right everyone, let's get to work."

After what seemed to Cecelia, far too few directions, the cast assembled to their opening places on the stage.

"We will run through the first scene," Percival announced, gesturing Cecelia to her place. "Now Sis— uh, Amber, you know the songs, so just try to follow Vivian and Daniel's lead with the stage movements. They will not mind helping you. Are you ready?"

Cecelia nodded, with a confidence she was far from feeling.

Julian watched critically from the wings as the new Justine started across the stage rather stiffly toward her abigail as the narrator opened the scene.

"Come downstage, a little more Amber," Levison directed. Cecelia hesitantly turned the wrong way and Percival quickly added, "No, uh, downstage, this way." He gestured to her proper place.

The duke's countenance tightened. The chit acted as though she had never been on a stage before! Despite her beauty, Levison wasn't going to get by with giving some novice the lead, just to get the play to open.

"I should not worry, sir, I expect she's just nervous," Daniel noticed the duke's expression and tried to reassure him, though the actor didn't appear too happy himself about a leading lady who didn't seem to even know stage directions.

"I should hope so," the duke murmured quietly, as Daniel left to take his own place on stage.

The duke relaxed somewhat on hearing the singer's rich baritone fill the theater in the tale of the star-crossed lovers. At least Levison had a good male lead in Robert. And the actress playing Sophia, she was a pretty wench with a light, clear voice, quite suited to the supporting role of Justine's abigail. Levison had done well casting these two. They could likely carry the play, if this Amber had even a passable voice.

Percival moved in front of the duke, not even noticing him, as he anxiously signaled Cecelia to get ready for Justine's opening aria.

Levison didn't seem to have much confidence in his protégé—the duke frowned at Percival's obvious tension, but his frown vanished as the clear strains of the most beautiful soprano he recalled ever hearing, wafted across the stage.

Even Daniel missed his cue, and merely stood staring at Cecelia for several long seconds as Justine's hauntingly beautiful opening lament filled the silent theater. Then a delighted Daniel joined in and their two voices seemed to entwine in the hot summer afternoon, much as the lovers themselves might.

The whole cast was wreathed with tearful smiles as they applauded enthusiastically when Cecelia's poignant solo ended the scene a few minutes later.

Percival unabashedly wiped away his own tears. "Ah, love, you have just made my fortune," he murmured softly and was startled as another voice from behind him agreed.

"Yes, I expect she has. Congratulations, Levison." The duke patted the younger man on the shoulder. "You have done quite well."

Chapter Three

"Now Miss Amber, I ain't into no fancy cooking but I'll be more than 'apply to try my 'and at whatever you wish if this don't please you." Martha continued a worried disclaimer as she bustled about serving her mistress's dinner the next evening.

"This smells quite wonderful, Martha," Cecelia soothed the anxious woman. "I am certain it shall be fine."

"Miss Amber." The old butler quite properly held her chair for her.

"Thank you, Wally." Cecelia smiled. The servants had outdone themselves trying to please her.

In fact, Cecelia was quite pleased with both Martha and Wally, as much so, as apparently they were with her, both of them treating her almost like royalty despite her presumed trade.

Cecelia smiled on recalling Martha's initial reaction to discovering she was in Percival's play.

"Y'er sayin' y'er an *actress!* But—you seem such a

lady!'' the cook had declared in horror before catching herself and profusely apologizing.

Cecelia knew even Wally had been shocked at the discovery though, more appropriately, he had refrained from making comment.

"Mr. Levison will not be dining with you after all this evening, Miss Amber?" the butler interrupted her thoughts. He had heard the young man say he would return and feared Martha had forgotten to put out a second place setting.

"No. Percival had a previous engagement, however he intends to stop by later," Cecelia supplied absently.

Something about Wally's overly bland "Yes, miss" drew Cecelia's attention and she glanced up from her plate just in time to catch Martha's expression before the butler's hard look set the woman to busily gathering up covers.

Realizing the servant's interpretation of Percival's *stopping by* later, Cecelia's face colored. Of course, that was what she had planned for people to think—that she was Percy's mistress, but somehow having this kindly couple think such of her was too appalling.

"Martha, wait a moment," she stopped the housekeeper's intended escape to the kitchen. "I would like to explain something to you and Wally."

"Miss, that is not at all—" the butler tried to stop her.

"No, please. Both of you."

The two came over reluctantly to stand before her.

"Can I trust both of you to keep something in utmost confidence?"

Cecelia didn't dare tell them her real name. She merely said she was from a country family in Cumbria but confided that Percival was actually her cousin, and briefly told them what had happened with his play.

"—as we were raised together, Percy is really more a brother to me, so there was no way I could let his play fail when Miriam ran off," she finished.

"Mr. Levison is your *cousin!* You must forgive us, Miss Amber—" Wally began in distress but Cecelia stopped him.

"No. I don't blame either of you in the least for your assumptions. In fact, that is what we intended." At their astonished look, she explained.

"Percival feared, thinking me an actress, some men might make, uh, well, unwelcome advances. So in order to discourage such a possibility, I decided to present the appearance of being Percy's lady friend, and therefore, unavailable. As no one knows me in London, it does not matter what they might think, but I just could not let you two believe that Mr. Levison and I were—well, you understand," she trailed off in embarrassment.

"Why miss," Martha raised the corner of her apron to swab at her eyes, "that there is the most beautiful thing I ever 'eard of anyone doing for some'un else! Risking y'er own good name to save Mr. Levison's future! Now, Wally didn't I tell you Miss Amber 'ad the kindest 'eart ever?"

The butler, a bit more sophisticated than his friend, looked at his employer in alarm. "Please pardon me, miss. I know it is not my place to offer counsel but—though it is very generous of you to help your cousin, I fear neither you nor Mr. Levison understand the—dangers to yourself in what you are doing."

"Danger?" Cecelia frowned. "I appreciate your concern, Wally, but I cannot imagine what there is to fear? Percival shall always be there when I am at the theater so surely, no one would suggest anything—untoward to me, thinking he is my—protector."

The butler shook his head in disbelief. "I have worked

for the nobility for years, miss, and am quite familiar with their ways. Mr. Levison is likely correct in believing the other actors would not approach you if they think you are his—uh, lady friend, but you can not trust noblemen to necessarily honor the relationships of persons they consider beneath their own station."

Cecelia smiled, certain the butler was just being overly cautious. "Well, I am sure there is no cause for alarm, but I promise you I shall be careful."

In her sitting room later, Cecelia explained to her abigail why she had told the servants about herself. "If you could have seen Martha's expression when I said Percival was coming back tonight—I just could not let it pass. I should have as soon allowed the rector to think I was stealing from the poor box!"

"Well, I have heard them whispering about in concern on you and Mr. Levison and been tempted to tell them myself, so I cannot blame you," Hannah admitted, setting aside a gown she had finished altering for the play. "I am sure you do not need to worry about them letting your secret out. I imagine either one of them would just about die for you or Mr. Levison as they're so grateful for being hired."

"Wally and Martha are dears, are they not?" Cecelia smiled. "I think even you have come to like them, though I know you were horrified when they first arrived."

Hannah laughed. "Who wouldn't have been? But you are right. You cannot help but like someone who tries so hard to please. I finally just had to tell Martha to stop, the poor woman would have worked herself to death cleaning and shining even after this place was spotless. And, despite his age, Mr. Wordsworth has certainly earned his keep. Did you notice he fixed that step out front today?"

"Did he?" Cecelia sat down and idly began pulling the pins from her hair. "I shall make sure to compliment him on it tomorrow." She shook her head and the thick auburn curls fell into rich disarray about her shoulders.

"I wonder what happened to Percival? He was supposed to come by tonight."

Hannah shrugged. "He probably forgot. You know how single minded he gets when he's working on that play."

"Indeed, I do!" Cecelia gave a wry laugh. "He almost forgot me at the theatre today. Well, if he does not arrive soon, I shall seek my bed, as it has been quite a long day." She glanced vaguely toward the bedroom. "Would you find my brush?"

"I will attend to your hair in just a few minutes but first I have some reservations about one of these gowns." She brought out a deep rose silk from the pile of costumes Percival had sent to be altered. "I think you had best try this one on."

"I thought you had all my measurement memorized," Cecelia joked, coming over. "Why, that is a lovely gown—" she began but stopped as Hannah held the offending dress up to herself. "Oh, I see. It appears the bodice is a bit low, does it not?"

"That is what I feared," Hannah agreed. "But slip it on. Maybe it is not as bad as it appears."

"My heavens!" Cecelia laughed a few minutes later, tugging at the front of the gown as Hannah fastened the long row of tiny buttons up the back. "Are you certain it isn't backwards? I believe more of me is out, than in!"

Hannah walked around in front of her mistress, and chuckled. "True, but it is *magnificent* on you!" She cocked her head inquisitively. "In fact, it is so lovely, it would almost be a shame to—"

"No." Cecelia cut her abigail off with a reproving look. "Kindly recall, I am only *playing* an actress. Now surely, you can do something to make this a bit more— decent?"

"Well," Hannah considered the matter a moment. "I may have some cream lace to match that in the sleeves. I expect a bit sewn into the bodice here should suffice—" she indicated the deeply cut décolletage. "I will go and see what I can find in my sewing box," she agreed, absently gathering up the dress Cecelia had been wearing as well as the pile of other costumes. "I'll take these with me to hang."

After she left, Cecelia crossed idly to the fireplace. She was just placing another log on the andirons when there was a knock at her door.

"Amber?"

"Come on in, Percy." Cecelia had become so accustomed to her new name that she paid no note to her cousin using it in private. "I feared you were not going to come by after all and—" she stopped on realizing her cousin was not alone.

"Forgive me for being late." Percival stepped into the sitting room. "Stanford had some matters he wished to discuss with me—very good news, in fact. I hope you do not mind that I brought him with me?"

Cecelia did mind, particularly in light of her current attire.

"Oh, uh, of course not," she managed, avoiding the duke's eyes as he entered the room. "Good evening, Your Grace."

Good God, the woman was even more beautiful than he'd suspected! The duke watched with shuttered eyes as Cecelia dropped into a curtsy before him, the profusion of amber curls cascading forward over a delightful exposure of creamy breasts. It was a pity Levison already had a liaison with her! Though how the playwright afforded a high-flyer like this one was a matter to pon- der—Julian smiled at the blush that flagged the young woman's cheeks when she finally raised her eyes to his.

"That is a—charming gown, my dear," Julian mur- mured, unexpectedly taking her hand. "Rose is quite becoming to you."

"Thank you," Cecelia responded automatically, her thoughts diverted from the embarrassing dress to the touch of the duke's lips brushing the backs of her fingers as he bent over her hand. Cecelia's own lips curved unconsciously into a smile as a wave of the duke's thick hair fell incongruently over his chiseled forehead when he straightened.

Julian drew his breath in quietly on catching that smile. The woman was an enchantress! He gave a surrep- titious glance at the playwright but the young man seemed to have noticed nothing untoward.

"You will never believe this, love," Percival began enthusiastically, "Stanford has offered to be my patron! He has invited me to produce my plays at Barcelly all of next year."

"Why, that's wonderful! How very kind of you, Your Grace."

The lovely eyes looking up at him in unaffected plea- sure, distracted the duke so that his reply was a bit delayed. "Oh, not at all. I have full confidence in Levison's plays—and his cast," he added with a warm look.

Cecelia suddenly became aware that he yet held her hand, and quickly withdrew it. "Um, would you care for tea, Your Grace?"

"No, thank you."

Julian found himself even more intrigued at her again, heightened color. He had never known a courtesan to blush so convincingly. Could it be the woman was as new to the demimonde, as he suspected she was to the stage?

"Actually, Levison suggested we might impose upon you to read a scene from *Rue de L'amour*, as we have determined that shall be the first play of next season's billet," Julian continued smoothly.

"Well, I do not mind reading, of course," Cecelia gave her cousin a covert look, "but as you know, Percival, I have not committed to being here for the next season."

"Amber has considered going back to act in France after this production," Percival quickly advised, anxious that Stanford might have second thoughts on sponsoring the next season without her, at least until he had proven his play before an audience. "But I may be able to change her mind when she sees how well *Justine* is received."

"Indeed? Let us hope you are successful." Julian smiled, applying his own meaning to Levison's words. So *that* was how the chap had lured the chit into his protection—with promise from the play's future receipts. He might keep her in the play, but unfortunately, if Levison hoped to keep the woman for himself personally, he was incredibly naive. Regardless how successful, no playwright could ever match the *carte blanche* London bloods would be willing to offer for a choice morsel like this one—that is, were they given the chance. The duke toyed with a rather appealing idea as he watched Cecelia. He had determined to never take another mistress after that irritating incident with Rosalind, but this woman was different somehow.

"Please, have a seat, Your Grace." Percival waved the duke to a wing back chair. "We shall read from the third act, as that is the climax of the play." He drew the sheets from a folder.

"Forgive me, my dear, but I have only the one copy." The duke was rather surprised at a twinge of jealousy when Percival casually drew the woman closer to share the one set of sheets.

"You start with the second paragraph, where Rachelle opens. I'll read Etienne's part."

"Percival, for heaven's sake, I should have to climb in your pocket to read it there." Cecelia laughed, as her cousin peered at the script nearsightedly. "Here," she casually reached into his inside pocket and pulled out a pair of reading glasses. "Put on your spectacles."

The young man put on the glasses, giving her a reproving look. "Very well, then you can hold the script." He tried to hand the sheets to Cecelia.

"Oh, posh! I do not bite, Percy," Cecelia merely moved closer. "Now, where did you say I start?"

Neither noticed the duke's smile, as he watched Cecelia's teasing camaraderie with Percival. The woman was delightful—as unpretentious and at ease with Levison as though they were family. Even outside of the obvious benefits, her company would be enjoyable, Julian thought, coming to a decision. There was, of course, the matter of Levison. He rather liked the young playwright and should not wish to embarrass him by simply taking the woman. But surely they could come to some equitable arrangement, the duke decided, especially as Levison seemed surprisingly oblivious to his mistress's charms.

It never even occurred to the duke that Amber might refuse him. Julian's confidence was not based on conceit for it was an accepted premise in the muslin trade that the prime articles always went to the deepest pocket. The duke could obviously better the playwright's offer to the wench, or for that matter, even those overtures any of his peers might consider making.

". . . that ends the third act. Shall we continue, Your Grace?"

Percival's question brought the duke's mind back to the reading, to which in truth, he had been paying little attention. "No, no. That was excellent," he complimented anyway having determined the play's worth in his previous scanning of the script. "I shall look forward to the production." He stood, to take his leave. "I quite enjoyed your reading, Amber." He turned to Cecelia. "You will be perfect for the part of Rachelle."

"Thank you, Your Grace. However, please recall I may not yet be in London next season," Cecelia reiterated firmly.

"Oh, I am sure we shall be able to come to terms pleasing enough to entice you to remain with us."

Uneasy at something in the duke's warm smile, Cecelia made a non committal murmur, as she escorted the two men to the door.

"Goodnight, Your Grace. Will I see you in the morning, Percy?"

Percival turned back. "Oh, actually I was just escorting His Grace out. Could you wait up for me a few moments, love? I needed to speak to you about some things."

The duke's jaw tightened. The young pup wasn't as oblivious to the woman as he appeared! In light of his decision to take Amber into his own keeping, Julian found the thought of the playwright returning to her that night quite annoying. "Mr. Levison, I had hoped I might induce you to accompany me to my club. There are some other matters I had wished to discuss with you," the duke said, deciding to make an *offer* to the playwright for Amber that very evening.

Chapter Four

"Your Grace!" Percival twisted on the soft leather squabs of the duke's carriage, to stare at the other man in disbelief. "Surely you jest, sir!"

"Not at all, Mr. Levison." Julian was encouraged rather than perturbed, at the younger man's shock since the figure he'd named had been quite generous. "Please understand, this is simply a business offer, one man to another. I certainly expect to recompense you for any inconvenience." He paused, but when the playwright merely stared at him in stunned silence, added wryly. "If that amount is not sufficient, you may name your own, for, as you've doubtless guessed, the woman quite intrigues me."

"The *woman intrigues you?*" Percy gasped before he recalled that this man was only believing the subterfuge he and Cecelia themselves had created. With considerable effort, Percival regained his decorum. "I am afraid your suggestion is quite impossible, sir. There is absolutely no way that I would ever consider such a thing!

I am—quite content with my relationship with Amber and have no desire to—to give her up for any amount of—compensation," he stammered, horrified at the whole conversation. "Not to mention that she would be aghast at such a proposal!" he added with a shudder, imagining Cecelia's reaction should she ever get wind of the duke's offer to buy her from him.

Julian smiled at the young man's naiveté in the way's of courtesans. "Come now, Percival," he appealed to the playwright's ego by using his given name. "It is quite obvious that Amber cares for you, and you for her, but it is equally obvious that there is no real passion involved, at least on your part. In fact tonight, though she'd gowned herself particularly to entice you, you scarcely seemed to notice."

"Entice me?" Percival looked puzzled a moment before the duke's meaning occurred to him and he flushed scarlet. "Sir, I am appalled, that you should think such!"

"Think?" Julian looked at him in amusement. "You give yourself too little credit, my friend. Why else might your ladybird have been gowned so delightfully?"

"That gown Amber wore is one designed for the third act of *Justine.*—Doubtless she was just trying it on," Percival advised him archly.

Julian merely chuckled. "Indeed? Just trying it on exactly when she was expecting you to arrive? Cut line, Levison, we are mature men. That gown with its intriguing décolletage, was chosen to be seductive, and forgive me for admitting it, but I found it quite effective."

"Seductive!" Percival glared at the other man in outrage, this time totally forgetting Cecelia was supposedly his mistress. "You admit you—you were—thinking—! I cannot believe you would be even *thinking* such in a lady's home!"

The duke's eyebrows raised. "Come, Mr. Levison. A *lady's* home? Is that not the residence you are providing her for her favors?"

"Well, I—I—" Percy sputtered in confusion.

"I expect Amber is your first mistress, is she not?" Taking Percival's expression as answer, the duke smiled. "My young friend, I fear you are dabbling in realms which you really should not. You are too much the idealist to be involving yourself with the demimonde. I dare say you should be much happier finding some sweet country girl to wed."

"I am married!" Percival snapped, annoyed at the duke's patronizing tone. "And to a very sweet county girl!"

The duke's look turned cold. "I had taken you more for a man of honor, Mr. Levison. If you are wed, then why are you not with your wife rather than spending your blunt on some Cyprian? Or is this the only way you could convince Amber to act in your play?"

"No—I didn't." Percival was momentarily thrown on the defensive. "It was Cec—uh, Amber's idea to play the lead in *Justine* when Miriam left. Besides," he regathered himself, "I must say, I find it rather astonishing to be called on my actions, by you, *Your Grace*. Is it not a known fact that most gentlemen of the ton, have both wives and mistresses? And furthering the point, your own intentions toward Amber seem scarcely honorable!"

The duke's eyes narrowed dangerously. "My intentions toward Amber are certainly as honorable as an actress, already accepting the protection of another man, can possibly expect. And, as for being married, you are correct in much of nobility's behavior, but certainly not all. Personally, I consider marriage a sacred covenant and would never dishonor my wife, had I one, by keeping a mistress as well."

"How commendable," Percival observed dryly, reaching for his satchel. "You are wrong where Amber and I are concerned, but I have no intention of arguing the matter. Now, as I can only assume your interest in being my patron was but a ruse to gain yourself an intriguing new mistress, we can dispense with any further business discussions. If you would be so kind as to have your coachman let me out?"

The duke considered the young man in surprise, not sure at all what to make of him. "No wait," he said, determined to take another tack. "It is painfully obvious I have been ham-fisted in my approach to this matter. Please, accept my apology, Mr. Levison. I had no idea you felt so strongly about the woman."

"I expect you would be quite surprised at my feelings for the woman," Percival retorted coolly.

The duke sighed. "Forgive me, I have again been insensitive. I can understand your caring for Amber, as she is quite as charming as she is lovely. But surely you can grant that under the circumstances, my assumptions were understandable?"

Percival begrudgingly had to agree. "I suppose, taking into allowance that you are not personally acquainted with the lady in question."

"That is true, but I beg you concede that I am, in all likelihood, more knowledgeable than you about such ladies in general?"

"Doubtless. But your knowledge, however vast," Percival added sarcastically, "is not applicable to Amber."

The duke merely shrugged. "Mayhaps. But, in the past I have found the demimonde to be quite vulnerable to titled nobility, for the prestige as well as access to deeper pockets. Are you quite certain your Amber might not be tempted by such?''

"I assume this is your tactful way of suggesting Amber might willingly come to you, Your Grace?'' Percival asked wryly.

"Can you not conceive such a possibility?'' the duke asked carefully.

To his surprise, Percival chuckled.

Thinking of Cecelia's attitude toward nobility in general, and particularly those with inherited fortunes, Percival innocently offered the duke the opportunity he sought. "No affront intended, Your Grace, but no, I cannot conceive of such. And were I in your place, I shouldn't try to sway Amber with your fortune or most certainly not, your title, as I assure you, you would achieve naught but an embarrassing set down.''

"A most daunting prospect,'' the duke drawled pausing for a moment. "Perhaps you are correct but, just as a matter of interest, if Amber *were* to decide to change protectors, would you forbid her?''

"Me, forbid her?'' Percival considered the idea in some astonishment. "My dear sir, forgive me, but you again exemplify your innocence of that lady. No one forbids her *anything,* least of all, myself. In fact, I fear on a lamentable number of occasions, she has convinced me to sanction her own quite rackety notions,'' he added, morosely thinking of the current situation.

"Ah, I see.''

Feeling uneasy at something in the duke's smile, Percival felt compelled to add further dissuasion. "Despite my words, sir, Amber is as you say, under my protection and I will not stand by and allow anyone to try to pressure her with unwelcome proposals,'' he commanded with a reasonable attempt at sternness.

"Of course. That is quite understandable. You may

have my word, Mr. Levison, that I would never attempt
to coerce Amber, or any female, to accept such a proposal were they in the least reticent.'' The duke nodded,
confident that no such pressure would be needed.
''Now, if we might consider that rather difficult matter
settled,'' he continued smoothly, ''I did wish to discuss
the next season in greater detail with you, if you are yet
willing?''

After a brief hesitation, Percival allowed himself to be
mollified and entered into the new subject innocently
assuming the duke had abandoned his previous quest.

Chapter Five

"Miss Amber," one of the dressers nudged Cecelia, during a brief break in the rehearsal the next evening. "That duke didn't take his eyes off you for a moment during these last two acts."

"Oh fustian," Cecelia said lightly as several cast members turned to listen in interest. "The gentleman is merely following the progress of the play, Nelly, since he is sponsoring it."

"Well, he's been following your part real close all day long," the girl giggled, unconvinced. "And I'd wager, all it'd take is a flit of your skirt, Miss Amber, and you'd have that 'un on the string if you'd a mind!"

Cecelia ducked her head over a presumed errant thread on her sleeve, to hide her flush. "Nelly! His Grace is quite above such as that, I'm sure. Besides, as you well know, I am perfectly content in my—relationship with Mr. Levison," she managed with reasonable aplomb.

"Mr. Levison is fortunate to command such loyalty!"

Vivian joined in the teasing not even bothering to contest the duke's being above such. "But lud, if I had a titled swell like that one ready to give me the wink, our playwright would be out on the cobblestones!"

Cecelia's lips tightened indignantly on her cousin's behalf. "Percival is a kind and wonderful man! That's much more important than the duke's title or fortune!"

Vivian merely laughed. "I agree, Mr. Levison, is a good cove, but the duke—now there's a *man* for you!" She nodded to where Julian stood speaking to Percival. "Look at that, see what I mean?"

Unthinking, Cecelia followed Vivian's direction and her gaze was caught by a fascinating display of muscular thigh bulging under skin-tight trousers, as the duke placed his foot on a handy stool to check a scratch on his Hessians.

"No spider-shanks there!" Vivian sighed deeply. "Can you just imagine how your duke will look without—"

"Vivian!" Cecelia shook herself from her own unseemly inspection to stop the actress in shock.

Hearing Cecelia's admonition to Vivian, Julian glanced up. His laconic grin as he removed his boot from the stool indicated he had doubtless guessed the subject of their interest.

Cecelia looked quickly away, mortified at being caught gawking at him.

Despite her denial to Nelly, Cecelia had noticed the duke, rather surprisingly, remained all day in the front row seat. Several times she had covertly glanced out to find him watching her with a look in those lazy hooded eyes that created alarming flutters in her midsection.

Unbeknownst to Cecelia, Julian had been quite encouraged by those several glances, she thought he hadn't noticed. Doubtless Percival's presence made the chit reticent to show it overtly, the duke determined comfortably, but contrary to Levison's naive assumptions, she *was* interested! Confident that she only hesitated at his sanctioning her interest, the duke proceeded with his plan.

"All right everyone." Percival came back on the stage, after Stanford departed a few minutes later. "Let's go finish this last scene. Then the duke has arranged a surprise for you."

"A surprise?"

"Stanford said he realized how hard you have all been working to pull this play together and wished to compensate you for some of the long hours. He's invited everyone, including the stage hands, to his home for dinner this evening!"

"Dinner at the duke's?" Vivian gasped at that unprecedented offer. "Are you bamming us?"

"Not at all," Percival laughed. "In fact, he is sending his own carriages over at seven, for those of you without transportation."

"Oh my, but what of our costumes?" one of the actresses began anxiously.

"That is of no concern," Percival assured her. "Stanford realizes you were rehearsing in dress, and said you should come as you are. Now, I think we'd best get on with this scene, if we are to finish our work in time."

The flickering gas lights had been lit along Pall Mall as the carriages converged on one of the street's most elegant houses.

Much to their credit, the array of footmen who came out to open carriage doors never batted an eye on finding they were handing down painted ladies of the theater.

The duke himself met them in the grand marbled entrance. "Welcome, my friends. Mrs. Hartwell, will take your wraps." He indicated his waiting housekeeper.

"You know Percival," Cecelia whispered aside to her cousin as they were ushered into an enormous parlor, "I am beginning to come over to your mind."

"In reference to what?" He glanced at her curiously.

"The nobility. I believe you were right, all titled men are not alike."

"You are referring to Stanford?" Percival followed her discrete gesture in surprise. His own recent experience with the duke having almost swayed him to his cousin's jaded notion of the aristocracy.

"Of course. Just look at him." She motioned to where the duke was personally greeting each of the cast members. "He is as gracious with the cast as though they were peers. And even his dress is casual, in deference to our costumes," she added approvingly. "That shows amazing thoughtfulness, especially for a male."

"Cecelia?" Percival looked at her in concern. "You would not be allowing yourself to develop feelings for this man would you?"

"Percy!" Cecelia chastised, though avoiding his eyes. "What a thing to suggest!"

Percival frowned, not at all convinced, but he didn't dare tell her what he knew, least she accost the duke outright in her fury. "Sissy, please do not forget that the duke believes you to be but an actress. I have noticed he has been watching you an awful lot, and I am concerned that he might start to have—well, unacceptable thoughts about you."

Cecelia merely smiled. "Oh, you need not worry, Percy. The duke has been nothing but polite to me. Besides, remember, he thinks I belong to you."

"Uh, Sissy, there is something you should know—" Percival began anxiously but his cousin stopped him.

"Shh, here comes the duke now."

"Ah, and here are my two guests of honor!" Stanford smiled. "Levison, I must admit I had my doubts at first that you could save this production after Miriam left. But now, I have full confidence in the play's success with our Amber here as its leading lady." Much to Percival's concern, the duke took Cecelia's hand and tucked it proprietarily about his arm. "Come, my dear. Both of you," Julian remembered to include Percival. "Let us find Daniel. I must propose a toast."

Rather alarmed on finding herself the object of the duke's full attention *and* that she was quite enjoying it, Cecelia took the first opportunity to move from his side.

"Excuse me, gentlemen, but Vivian said she wished to speak to me," she allowed vaguely, avoiding the duke's eyes as she left him with Daniel and Percival after a few minutes.

"Would you care for some ratafia?"

"No thank you," Cecelia declined the young maid's offer some time later. Dinner had still not been called and the numerous, loud toasts from the exuberant cast, on top of the grueling day's rehearsals had given her a pounding headache.

"Are you all right, miss?" the maid asked in concern on noticing the young woman's pallor.

"No, actually I fear I have a dreadful headache," Cecelia admitted. "I do not suppose there might be somewhere quiet I could sit for a few moments, perhaps with a cool cloth?"

"Of course, miss," the girl replied sympathetically. "If you would, come with me."

Julian happened to glance up just as Cecelia and the maid left the room and shortly excused himself from the rest of the party.

"You'll not be disturbed up here." The maid led Cecelia up the stairs to an antechamber set aside for the females of the cast to rest and repair themselves. "No one but the other ladies will come in here, so if you'd like I will loosen your gown a bit so you'll be more comfortable."

"Yes, thank you," Cecelia agreed in relief, turning to allow the girl to undo the top buttons of the snug dress.

"Now, miss, perhaps if you lay down on that chaise for a few minutes." The maid dampened a cloth in cool water of a waiting ewer and brought it to her. "Here, this should help. I will go and have the housekeeper prepare a tisane for you."

"Thank you." Cecelia settled appreciatively on the soft lounge, placing the damp cloth over her forehead and burning eyes.

Her headache already dulling a few minutes later, Cecelia paid scant attention to the murmuring of voices outside her door.

"One of the young misses had a bit of a migraine, Your Grace," the duke's young maid advised him on his inquiry. "I was just bringing her a tisane."

"I see." The duke smiled to himself. He had been hoping for just such a chance to be alone with Amber. "I will take that in to her."

"But sir, she is lying down and—" as the duke merely raised a brow the young maid blushed and handed him the glass.

"Thank you. You will see that we are not disturbed?"

"Yes, Your Grace." The flustered girl bobbed a curtsy

and retreated to waylay any other guests at the base of the stairs.

Julian confidently entered the room. "I have brought you a remedy for your headache, my dear."

Startled to hear the duke's voice instead of the maid's as she'd expected, Cecelia snatched the cloth from her eyes and sat up, struggling to straighten her gown. "Your Grace? What are you—"

"Do not be concerned, my sweet," the duke said over his shoulder as he carefully closed the door. "I'm pleased that we've a chance to be alone." He turned with a warm smile, however both his smile and words faltered when he looked at her.

"Your Grace, I must insist that you leave immed—" Cecelia's outraged order was cut off as the duke burst into laughter.

"I fail to see what you find amusing about this situation, sir!" Cecelia snapped, her initial alarm turning to irritation at his bizarre reaction.

"Forgive me, my dear," Julian attempted to stifle his mirth, but was undone when Cecelia stood, raising her chin haughtily. "I just" his words again dissolved into chuckles at her glare. "Here, take your medicine, before I spill it."

"Sir, I believe you are into your cups!" Cecelia indignantly took the glass he offered and turned to sit it on the table. "Now, I would appreciate it if you would leave." She stopped, frowning down at the previously white cloth she'd had over her eyes, now stained with bright blue, black and green. "What on earth? *Oh no!*" Cecelia groaned, suddenly realizing what had happened. She had forgotten she was still wearing the heavy theatrical make-up when the maid brought her the wet cloth.

She picked up the bit of material, glancing reluctantly

at the duke. "I suppose this means that my—make-up is—?"

"Yes, I am afraid so," the duke managed. Placing his hands on her shoulders, he turned her to the mirror.

"Oh, good heavens!" Cecelia stared in horror at the blotches of black kohl now mixed with blues and greens of eye make-up, running in spikes down her cheeks.

"I do apologize," the duke chuckled from behind her, "but you must admit, the sight is a bit—disconcerting."

Cecelia's lips tightened as she tried to regain some sense of dignity. "Disconcerting? What is *disconcerting*, Your Grace, is why you should be here at all, in chambers set aside for your female guests?" Yet loath to turn, Cecelia glared at the duke in the mirror.

Julian was momentarily nonplussed. "I had thought it an opportunity for us to—um—that is—I had hoped—"

Cecelia's lips twitched as the duke faltered, his gaze moving over her blotchy face in marked consternation.

"Well, Your Grace?" She almost managed a haughty tone.

"Um, I am afraid, my dear—that I do not think that I can—"

The duke's eyes met hers in the mirror and the ridiculousness of the situation was too much for Cecelia. A giggle escaped her primly pressed lips.

"Sir, you should be ashamed," she tried once again but at the duke's chagrined expression, Cecelia gave up and dissolved into laughter. "Oh my!" She leaned weakly back against the duke's chest, the tears running down her face revitalizing the make-up into new streams.

"Are you sure you don't want to—" Cecelia made as

though to turn toward him but the duke's arms wrapping about her from behind, stopped her.

"No—please—my valet would kill me," he managed amidst rumbling laughter as she pretended to struggle.

"But Your Grace—here you have me all alone—"

"What in heaven's name is going on in here?" The duke's housekeeper burst into the room. Hearing the commotion, she had come from the linen room just down the hall, thus missing the young maid standing guard.

"Oh, forgive me, Your Grace!" The woman stopped in alarm as Julian and Cecelia sprang apart. "I didn't realize—"

To his credit, the duke calmly addressed the woman. "That is quite all right, Mrs. Hartwell. Perhaps you can help. Miss Amber seems to have a problem with her—" he glanced down at Cecelia and had to stop. "That is, as you can see—"

Cecelia giggled and the duke simply gave up.

"Here you tell her," he laughed, pushing Cecelia toward the astonished housekeeper and still chuckling, strode from the room.

"Dinner is served, Your Grace," Ayers, Stanford's butler announced staidly, as the huge teak doors to the dining room were swung open.

Percival was considerably relieved when the duke carefully avoided Cecelia to offer his arm to the delighted Vivian as her escort into the dining room. Percival had feared the duke might take the opportunity of having Cecelia in his home to make advances toward her, but obviously Stanford had determined not to further pursue his quest where Amber was concerned.

For his cousin's part, though previously proven to be

correct, Cecelia considered her own concerns about the duke's intentions were now comfortably laid to rest. After that hilarious end to what was, doubtless, at least a prelude to seduction, Stanford would surely not consider her in that light again. In fact, it appeared throughout the evening he could scarcely look at her without breaking into chuckles, a predilection scarcely conducive to amorous interludes.

Both Percival and Cecelia's optimism concerning the duke's changed motives were unfortunately baseless. In fact, delighted with her sense of humor, Julian was more determined than ever that he should have Amber.

She could not now help but understand his intentions, the duke concluded, and from the few moments he'd held her in his arms, he gathered she had no protest. Now comfortably assuming the matter all but settled, Julian but awaited an appropriate time to bring her over under his own protection.

"Bexton, she is the most delightful female I have ever encountered," Julian confided to a friend at White's the following evening. "Quite different from the usual in mind, as well as being astonishingly lovely. Why with careful dressing, the auburn-haired chit could easily pass for a lady."

"You don't say. Hmm," the earl grinned. Flipping open a small jeweled case he took a delicate pinch of snuff. "And, when are you going to let me meet this new bit of fluff in the muslin market?"

The duke raised a brow. "Never, is most likely. I do still recall returning from my country estate to find you and that young buck Eddings enjoying yourselves with my last mistress."

"My dear fellow," his friend archly declared, "if I correctly recall, your main complaint on the episode seemed not to be with your ladybird, but rather that we had also imbibed a quantity of your private stock of port."

"The devil!" Julian remembered, frowning. "And, I recall you gave me your vow that you would replace it. It's been well past a year."

Bexton gave the duke a pained look. "Oh really, Stanford. Are you that done up that you must charge your friends for a bit of libation taken while entertained in your home?"

Julian laughed. "You are incorrigible, Bexton."

"Yes, it is true," the earl contentedly agreed. "Though, speaking of entertainment, we are all quite looking forward to the opening night of your young protégé's play."

The duke did not respond.

"You never did say who Levison found to play the title role after his bird-witted lead took French leave on him?"

"It is no one you would know. A new actress." The duke finished his drink determining it was time for him to take his leave.

Bexton grinned in sudden understanding. "Ah, now I would not suppose this new actress has any connection to the delightful female you were discussing earlier?"

Stanford coolly considered the other man for a moment. "Bexton, I really must introduce you to my tailor. I am surprised that Raggett allowed you to enter here in that waistcoat."

The earl chuckled to himself, as he watched Julian leave. "So, my dear old friend, you were going to secure this new *fille de joie* for your own stable without even allowing your friends an opportunity at her? That seems scarcely sporting! Perhaps I should venture out and see for myself how rehearsals for *Justine* are fairing?''

Chapter Six

"All right everyone, take your places," Percival directed the cast.

"I can't believe your duke isn't here for the final dress rehearsal," Vivian remarked to Cecelia as they assembled on the stage.

Cecelia glanced out to the empty front seat with a feeling suspiciously close to disappointment. Oddly, since their hilarious liaison, she had begun to feel quite comfortable with him—as a friend, of course, Cecelia told herself.

"Stanford is not *my* duke, Vivian," she corrected the other actress though she knew it would do little good. The cast had obviously made up their mind about the duke's intentions.

"Oh come now, Amber, after he comes here every single day and just watches you? Daniel said the man is merely biding his time before he makes you an offer. Likely, the duke doesn't want to risk upsetting Levison before the play opens since he has invested so much in it.''

Fortunately, at that moment Percival had the musicians begin, cutting off further conversation.

Near the end of the first act, Percival noticed a small group of gentlemen enter but didn't recognize them as they took seats in the rear of the theater. Perhaps Stanford had made it after all and not wished to interrupt them by coming forward.

While the actors were taking their places for the second act, Percival went to the back of the theater, but found the duke was not among the group of men.

"Good afternoon, Mr. Levison." A tall, fair-haired gentleman stood as Percival approached and introduced himself, "I am Bexton." The man didn't bother with his title. "We all are friends of Stanford's. He had said we might come join him to listen to the rehearsal, that is, if you don't mind?"

"Of course not," Levison innocently agreed. "Unfortunately, the duke sent a message that he could not be here today. There is some problem at his estate, I believe. But you are welcome to remain, in fact, I am pleased to have an audience for the dress rehearsal. It provides the cast all the more encouragement to do well." The playwright smilingly gestured them to follow him. "Why don't you gentlemen come up closer to the front, where you can see better?"

"Pity Stanford had to miss this," Bexton said with a covert grin to his friends, as Levison escorted them to the closer seats. The earl had, of course, discovered Julian was riding out to his country estate, which was precisely why they had come to the theater today.

Bexton's friends, Adderly, Constock and Melton had all been equally eager to get a look at this new ginger-

hackled bit of muslin, especially when he had told them
Stanford had expressed such a profound interest in
her. The duke had quite the reputation for the class of
woman he even bothered with these days.

The cast couldn't have asked for a more appreciative
audience, and indeed, even excelled their previous performances.

"My God, I do believe I'm in love!" Adderly grinned
to the others as Cecelia's voice rang out sweetly. "I fear
I simply must have that for my very own."

"Well, aren't you the deep-one? You had best accept
that you shall have to satisfy your love elsewhere," Constock jestfully dismissed his friend's possibilities. "For
unfortunately, that songbird has just stolen my own
heart. And, as I've twice your income, I can obviously
bid higher."

"Gentlemen. Gentlemen. You *do* recall who brought
you here?" Bexton coolly surveyed his friends. "I have
first choice, and that lady shall be none but *mine.*"

"You had all best be certain the lady isn't Stanford's
before announcing any claims to her," Melton
remarked dryly. He had once had the misfortune of
accidentally angering the Duke of Stanford, and learned
first-hand that it was a most unwise thing to do. "Everyone knows you got away with running tame with Julian's
last mistress, Bexton, but only because he had grown
tired of the chit anyway. However, I suspect, he won't
stand idly by for a replay with a beauty like this. He will
surely be up to every rig."

Bexton merely smiled. "Ah, but there is something
none of you know." The group leaned toward Bexton.
"She isn't under Stanford's protection, as yet. Actually,
I have discovered the playwright, Levison, is keeping
her."

"What? *Levison?*" The others looked at him in utter disbelief.

"Yes. Apparently, that is the reason why Julian has held off. Didn't want to upset the chap before opening night. And, until that ducal seal is stamped on the girl's millinery bills, well—" the earl elegantly shrugged his shoulders.

Much as Cecelia's butler had predicted, the fact that Amber was presumably the mistress of the playwright, was ignored by the young bucks.

"Well, Stanford's a fair man. I suppose if you get there before him, he might let you keep the chit," Melton cautiously allowed.

"*Let* me?" Bexton sniffed. "What could he have to say to it? As a gentleman he would never poach on another peer's property," the earl smugly declared, conveniently forgetting his own past transgression.

Much to the earl's surprise, and his friend's amusement, Bexton's initial advances on Amber met with naught but polite rejection.

"Thank you, Lord Bexton," Cecelia sweetly declined as she withdrew her hand from the admiring young earl's. "But, I fear Mr. Levison would never approve of you driving me home." She moved over by Percival and quickly tucked her arm into his. "Would you, my love?"

"What?" Percy looked down at his cousin in confusion as he'd been trying to straighten out a problem with the curtain hanging up and had heard none of the conversation.

Cecelia poked him in the ribs with her elbow. "I said, you would never allow this gentleman to take me home?" she gritted.

"Why love, if you wish to—" Percy began before

gasping as his cousin's elbow again attacked his already bruised ribs. "Oh, no. Of course not." He covertly rubbed his aching side. "Sir, Amber is my"—he tried sternly but couldn't quite manage the word—"that is— she and I—"

"Percy, you are such a dear!" Cecelia laughed as she turned to kiss his flushed cheek. "That is why I love you so very much." She glared at him as her back was to the others. "Mr. Levison is, of course, my protector," she murmured with demurely downcast eyes.

"You're going to take the chit from Stanford?" Adderly chortled once the four of them were outside the theater. "You can't even take her away from that pint-sized playwright!"

The earl calmly flipped open his snuff box. "My dear friends, I fear I did quite take that delectable little morsel a bit too much by surprise. She's obviously rather new at all this. But now she knows she has an option— it won't take the little ladybird long to come around." He delicately sneezed and dusted the excess snuff away with a lace handkerchief. "Especially, once I've sent over, shall we say, a sample of the benefits of changing nests?"

Constock laughed. "So, this Amber's new at this is she? I'll lay a pony that ladybird will be in Stanford's arms before the curtain is down on opening night. She isn't turning you down for that playwright, she just knows who's waiting in the wings."

"A pony, you say?" Melton joined in the bet good-naturedly. "I'll up it to two—Bexton's favor. I agree, the chit's a novice. You get her a pretty gewgaw before Stanford returns and she'll be in your pocket."

"No, I don't think—" The gentlemen continued

their friendly argument as they climbed back into Bexton's coach.

Cecelia had forgotten the presumptive lord by the time Percival dropped her back at the town house.

"You get a good night's rest now, Sissy," Percival counseled as he escorted her to the door.

"Are you not staying for dinner?" she asked, surprised when her cousin turned to leave.

"Thank you, but I really must go back to the Barcelly for a while longer."

"Percy, you're working much too hard." Cecelia looked at her cousin in worry. "Everything is fine with the play. You well know the final dress rehearsal was perfect. Even those friends of the duke's said it was marvelous."

"It did go rather well, did it not?" Percival happily agreed. "But you know how I am, Sissy. I shall not relax until opening night is behind us. However, you needn't worry, I'll not stay out long. I just want to check on that problem the stage hand had with the curtain lowering."

Cecelia frowned in concern as Percy directed his coachman back to the Barcelly. Well, after tomorrow night, if all went well, which she was sure it would, Percival would have his fortune made and she would not have to worry about him further, Cecelia decided, turning to enter her house.

"Good evening, Miss Amber." Wally was typically standing by for her hat and cape.

"Good evening. Heavens, what is that lovely scent?" Cecelia glanced up after unpinning her hat to see a bouquet of huge roses dwarfing the hall table. "Where did those come from?"

"From an admirer I expect, miss," the butler decreed

solemnly. "There are some other deliveries in the parlor."

"Some others?" Cecelia wandered over to the arrangement and pulled off the card, smiling. Perhaps they were from the duke, as he had known this was the final dress rehearsal—the seal, however, on the small card was unfamiliar.

"Roses, not near so lovely as the lady of *Justine,*" she read. "Your ever hopeful servant, Philip."

"Philip?" Cecelia had to think for a moment before she recalled that Philip was the Earl of Bexton's given name.

"Who is this Philip person?" Hannah came into the hall just then.

"Oh, just some young gentleman friend of the duke's that stopped by to see rehearsal today," Cecelia casually dismissed.

"He must have been quite impressed with the performance then," her abigail said wryly, directing Cecelia into the parlor.

"Oh, my goodness." Cecelia looked around at the room full of flowers. "Surely, these are not all from him?"

"Same seal on all the cards." Hannah handed her one from the nearest arrangement.

Cecelia glanced at the seal and chuckled. "Well, it would appear I have made a conquest!"

"I would be very careful, miss." Hannah frowned at her mistress's light dismissal of the matter as she picked up a velvet box from beside the flowers. "I strongly expect this young man plans to be the one making the conquest."

Cecelia looked askance at her maid before taking the jeweler's case and opening it. A rich, if rather gaudy, array of diamonds were clustered thickly on the necklace enclosed.

"These—these are real diamonds!" Cecelia raised the necklace to the light in amazement.

"One should certainly hope so, at least!" Hannah sniffed. "Though I can't say as I favor the style all that much."

"I cannot believe this." Cecelia stared at the card a moment in dismay before flipping it open.

"This is just a small token of my esteem," she read aloud, "but a sample of what your future holds."

"Future?" Cecelia's eyes widened in realization. "That—that coxcomb! Future, indeed! Wally!" she angrily called for the butler.

"Yes, miss, is something wrong?"

"I should say it is! Just look at this!" She displayed the necklace in contempt. "I cannot believe that young fool! I want you to have these immediately returned to the Earl of Bexton! And all of these—these flowers!"

"Of course, miss, but it is quite late and we haven't a coach," the butler worriedly reminded her. "I could try to track down a hackney."

Cecelia forced herself to be reasonable. "No, forgive me. I do not wish you roaming about at night. I can have Percival take care of it on the morrow. But you were right about these so-called gentlemen of the ton, Wally," she continued in distress. "This Bexton character actually expected I would accept this!" Her tone incredulous, she pointed to the necklace spilling from the open box. "Do you realize what that means?"

The butler coughed discreetly. "I, uh, image so, miss."

Cecelia continued, incensed. "He was scarce more than a half-licked pup—this Bexton! And he sends *these*, even after I firmly told him I belonged to Percival. Can you credit such a thing?"

The old butler carefully kept a straight face. "Quite outrageous behavior, Miss Amber. Uh, now I do believe Mrs. Cochran has dinner on the table?"

The Duke of Stanford's coachman was about to turn from the Marlebone highway toward Pall Mall when Julian happened to think how close they were to Amber's residence. "Thomas," he tapped on the roof and as his coachman pulled up, he leaned out to provide the different direction.

He had a perfect excuse to stop by the actress's home as it would be expected he might check on how the final rehearsal had gone. He could, of course, also say he'd thought to find Levison there, as it was the dinner hour. Though knowing the young playwright, Julian was quite certain that the man would be at the Barcelly theatre until quite late the night before opening.

His protégé could not be faulted for diligence. In fact, despite having such a tempting young female as Amber awaiting him, the man worked late almost every evening and then apparently went straight to his own bachelor quarters.

Julian was aware of Percival's activities because he had stationed one of his footmen, Morris, on Amber's street with instructions to waylay the playwright with an urgent summons to the duke, should he find the young man arriving for an evening tryst.

Even as they pulled before the actress's house, Morris, recognizing the duke's carriage, came over straight away.

"Y'er Grace." The man gave a tug at the corner of his cap as the duke stepped down from the coach.

"I do not see a carriage. Is Miss Amber inside?"

"Yes sir. That Levison fellow dropped 'er off a bit ago. I 'eard 'im say 'e was back off to that theater."

Julian smiled in satisfaction. "Thank you, Morris. You may take off the rest of the night. I do not suppose anyone else came by?" he asked at random.

"Well sir, a carriage did stop by, but it was a'for Miss Amber came 'ome. Seemed to be but a delivery, unloadin' a 'ole cartload of flowers."

The duke's eyes narrowed. "Flowers? You did not know the delivery man?"

"No Yer Grace. I believe 'e was in a lord's livery though, but as it was dark, I ain't rightly able to say which one."

Wally opened the door and was surprised to find the Duke of Stanford outside. "I am sorry, Your Grace, but if you are seeking Mr. Levison, I believe you will find him at the Barcelly Theater. He departed some time ago."

Though not invited, Julian walked past the man and into the small entry. "Levison's not here? Well, perhaps I might speak a moment with Miss Amber. I should like to see how the dress rehearsal went today." He handed the butler his coat and hat.

"Miss Amber is at dinner, Your Grace." The butler staidly waited, hoping the man would leave. Wally had no doubts on the duke's interest concerning his mistress, but didn't dare say anything to either her or Percival.

The duke frowned, his eyes taking in the huge vase of white, hot house roses in the hall. "Very well. I'll await her in the parlor. I don't suppose you might have any decent brandy in the house?"

The butler could think of no way to refuse. "Of course, Your Grace. I shall bring some right away and advise Miss Amber that you are here."

Julian entered the parlor and glared around at the other flowers. Doubtless, they were not from Levison. He had seen no sign that the playwright had ever bought Amber anything. He walked over to the table to check the card on an arrangement, but stopped as he glanced down.

"What in the—?" Bypassing the flowers, Julian picked up the card from the open box of diamonds and cursed softly to himself.

So Bexton was up to his old tricks again! Julian lifted the diamond necklace from the box in disgust. An expensive bauble, though tasteless! But then, perhaps an actress might like all that opulent glitter? The duke's jaw tightened as he yanked several cards from nearby flowers. They were all from Bexton? A reward perhaps for Amber's acceptance of an offer already made?

"Good evening, Your Grace—" Cecelia began but stopped in surprise as the duke turned coldly on her.

"I did not realize The Earl of Bexton was a friend of yours." The duke disdainfully gestured to the diamonds.

"I beg your pardon?" Cecelia's lovely chin raised indignantly.

"Or, should I have should have said lover?" The duke's tone was dangerously quiet.

"Sir!" Cecelia stared at him in momentary shock before fury took over. "How dare you? I only met the earl today at the dress rehearsal, which apparently *you* invited him to attend. That necklace as well as all of these"—she gestured to the room full of flowers—"hot house monstrosities, awaited me when I arrived home. I would have already sent his disgusting diamonds back to him, had I a means of doing so!"

The duke raised an aristocratic brow warningly, but he was so relieved at her words that he allowed her harsh reproving to pass without further sanction.

"I shall be pleased to return the diamonds to the earl for you." He tucked the velvet box into his breast pocket, his tone clearly suggesting she was testing his good nature.

"Thank you," Cecelia said curtly, annoyed yet further by his tone. "And, kindly advise *your friend* Bexton that I am not interested in his attentions!"

Julian gave her a long cool look, before walking pointedly away to gaze out the window. "Of course. Perhaps you would accept my apology," he said stiffly. "Though in truth, I did not invite Lord Bexton or the others to view the rehearsal, I shall see that he does not bother you again, if that is your wish."

"That is most definitely my wish," she stated to his back. When her words were met by naught but a frigid silence, Cecelia's inevitable sense of humor took over and she stifled a grin. It would seem she had annoyed "His Grace."

After another few long moments, she finally walked over beside the duke, determining it unwise to continue antagonizing her cousin's patron the night before opening.

"Please, forgive me, Your Grace," she said sweetly, "I was obviously being unfair to hold you accountable for your friend's actions and I suppose, your presumption was understandable. I fear that Lord Bexton's gall has me a mite wrought-up."

They were interrupted by a discreet knock on the door as Wally brought in the tea tray and the duke's requested brandy.

"Your Grace," Cecelia lay a hand beseechingly on the duke's arm, when he yet ignored her. "Wally has brought your brandy, sir, please do come and have a seat.''

Stanford hesitated another several moments as a lesson to her before finally allowing himself to be mollified. ''I suppose it is understandable you would be annoyed, particularly as you thought I had sent Bexton,'' he condescended, his tone yet cool.

''Well, Lord Bexton did say that you had invited them and I had no cause to disbelieve him.''

Julian glanced down at her in sudden understanding. It was a small wonder the woman had been so upset! She was as much as admitting she feared he had lost interest in her since he had not followed up on their rendezvous at his home. Doubtless, she'd assumed he had changed his mind, and sent friends in his stead! With a consoling smile, the duke tucked Cecelia's hand over his arm to lead her back to the couch. ''You have no need for concern, my dear. I assure you I did not give Bexton liberty to seek you out. In fact, I am quite annoyed to find he had the audacity to do so.''

Mentally fretting over the insult from the young lord, Cecelia missed the point of the duke's statement.

''Thank you, sir. I really cannot yet believe the presumption of that earl!'' she fumed. ''That he should dare imagine I would accept such a gift! Why, I scarcely even spoke a sentence to the man!''

Taking her further disavowal as but reassurance to himself that she hadn't sought the other man's attention, the duke patted her hand comfortingly. ''You need explain no further, Amber. I do not suspect that you encouraged Bexton, as I am quite familiar with his ways.''

''His ways?'' Cecelia seated herself on the couch as Wally set up the tea tray.

''It's nothing you need fret over further. I shall see

that the man does not approach you again," the duke dismissed, seating himself unasked, beside her. Julian considered a moment as the butler served his brandy and Cecelia's tea. Though he could keep Bexton away, doubtless others would be vying for a chance at Amber. Though, to avoid upsetting Levison, he had determined to be patient until the play was running smoothly before placing her under his own protection, he should make his intentions clear to her, least she be tempted by others.

"Now, Amber," the duke moved quickly to his purpose as soon as the butler left. "I realize I should have spoken to you sooner, after the happenings at my home the other night, to clarify my intentions but I—"

Cecelia, assuming the duke was set on apology, laughingly stopped him. "Please sir, I truly should prefer to put paid to that particular embarrassment! Suffice it to say, had I ever, I no longer have any misconceptions of your intentions."

The duke chuckled, applying his own interpretation to her words. "I should have known I could trust you to understand, my dear. However, I yet feel responsible. Perhaps you will allow me to compensate for causing you that embarrassment?" the duke offered, suddenly feeling quite generous.

"Compensate?" Cecelia looked up questioningly. "Sir, you needn't feel obliged—"

The duke waved her words away. "No. I have caused you distress. And in retrospect, I admit I was partially to blame for Bexton's advances. You see I happened upon him at my club with the thought of you yet fresh in my mind and couldn't resist telling him what an absolute delight my new leading lady was."

"Oh." Cecelia blushed, quite pleased at the compli-

ment despite the duke's obvious care in categorizing
his interest, she assumed to her part in the play.

"Levison has worked so hard on this play, that I hope
you will understand I do not wish to do anything to
upset him at this time, but if there is anything, anything
at all, you want—" Julian thought his offer clear but
the woman merely frowned up at him in confusion.

"Anything I want? What should I want?"

The duke sighed, deciding to try another tack. "My
dear, what I am saying is, that I am aware Levison is
somewhat pressed for funds until this play can produce
a worthwhile income, so there must doubtless be things
he cannot afford to give you. I wish you to feel comfortable in coming directly to me for anything you might—
need or wish."

"Your Grace, you are too generous." Cecelia smiled
at him warmly. The man was such a gentleman! Doubtless, he feared they might be in need of something, and
knew how loath Percy was to ask for more moneys.
"Though your offer is truly appreciated, I do not believe
it is necessary at this time."

The duke considered Cecelia in surprise. He could
not imagine any other of the demimonde bypassing
such *carte blanche.*

"Amber, it pleases me that you are so reticent, however such is not necessary. I do not mind at all advancing
you moneys, and, as *Justine* opens tomorrow night, it
shall not be for long that you need be concerned about
expenses," he said, thus discreetly allowing her to know
his intentions after the play's opening.

Cecelia was quite pleased with what she took to be
merely the duke's confidence in the play. She looked
up at him happily. "Are you truly convinced the play
shall succeed? Percival has been working so very hard
on it. I must admit I am worried on how he will manage

to keep on." She blushed at catching herself involving the duke in her personal matters. "Forgive me, sir. I forget myself. Percy is, of course, none of your concern."

"That is all right, my dear," Julian said, touched that she should share her anxiety over how her current lover would take her leaving. "Your regard for Levison is commendable, but I am convinced you need not worry. With you as its leading lady, the play cannot help succeeding, and I expect your Percival's pleasure in that, will make up for all else."

"You are too kind, sir." Cecelia blushed at his compliment. "I shall hope that *Justine* indeed meets up to your every expectation."

The duke chuckled softly, applying the name to the woman, rather than the play. "You've no need to concern yourself on that front either, my dear. I am quite certain I shall be more than satisfied."

The two smiled contentedly at one another, each encouraged by their own interpretation of the conversation.

Chapter Seven

After the fifth curtain call, the tired but exhilarated cast of *Justine* were finally allowed to retire to backstage, where their own personal congratulations began.

"Love, you were absolutely magnificent," Daniel enthusiastically grabbed Cecelia up and swung her about in delight.

Where Lady Cecelia Somersett could never have allowed such, Amber merely laughed in his arms. "And you, Dan!"

"Oops!" Daniel glanced up and winking at Cecelia, quickly set her down, as Percival and the duke approached. "I think I'd best go congratulate the others."

"Sissy, that was marvelous!" In his excitement, Percival absently reverted back to the name of their childhood, as he gathered her into a brotherly bear hug. "They loved it, pet. They absolutely loved it! You were all just unbelievably wonderful," he called to the other cast members, over their own cheers to their playwright-cum-manager. "Could you believe that audience reaction?"

"Yes." Cecelia laughed, brushing an errant lock of fair hair back from the young man's forehead. "How else would they react to such a brilliant play? Did I not tell you, you were wonderful, Percy?"

He grinned. "And I had simply assumed that was because you were biased, love. Stanford," he drew Cecelia over to where the duke stood watching, "could I ever have found a more perfect Justine?"

"Definitely not. But then, I can imagine no role in which Amber would be less than delightful."

Cecelia felt her heart skip strangely as Julian took her hand from Percival and raised it to his lips.

"You have the ton at your feet, my dear. Might I borrow your leading lady, Percival?" he asked, already tucking her hand over his arm.

Cecelia looked up askance at the duke as he led her to the large theater lobby where caterers were setting up a supper celebration.

"As these bucks are so determined to meet you," he nodded to a group of eager young lords awaiting them, "I thought it wiser if it were at my side," he explained, his protection thus discreetly denoted.

The naive young lady gave him a grateful look. "Thank you. I would certainly not wish for any more situations such as that with Lord Bexton!" Percival had been right all along about the nobility. Where there were some such as that Bexton character, there were others like Stanford, who were true gentlemen.

Julian patted her hand in satisfaction. "You are quite welcome. I haven't told you how I enjoyed your performance tonight, my dear. You have the talent and beauty to go to the top in the theater. Have you any plans for your next performance?"

Cecelia murmured her appreciation for his compliments though carefully avoiding the duke's eyes. "Actually, this production has been quite tiring. I should love to rusticate for a bit."

Since Amber was going to vanish forever once *Justine* ended its first run, Cecelia decided this was a good time to plant the first seeds of her withdrawal.

"Rusticate?" the duke questioned.

"Yes. As London is so terribly hot just now, I had aspirations of mayhaps—retreating to some quiet little place in the country for the rest of the summer," Cecelia elaborated, feeling vaguely guilty lying to the duke. But then Somersett was quiet and in the country, though describing the huge manor as little was doing it a bit brown.

"Hmm." The duke considered the matter a moment. He had planned to establish her in his Bay Street property, but she had suggested this place in the country in such a pretty way.

Actually, Julian decided, he liked the idea of her not working for awhile. He shouldn't have to be planning his visits around some theater schedule.

"Very well," he nodded agreement after a moment. "I shouldn't expect such a place will be too hard to find."

When Cecelia looked up askance at his odd comment the duke merely smiled at what he took to be her surprise on his easy approval.

"Actually, I much prefer the country myself. In fact, Stanford, my country seat, is where I spend most of my time. It is on the East Sussex coast but a short distance from Brighton. Have you ever been in that area?" the duke asked absently, thinking of several cottages convenient to his estate he might procure for her.

"Oh yes." Momentarily forgetting her role Cecelia

happily recalled her favorite relative who lived along the Sussex coast. "I enjoyed many a childhood summer on the beach at Starleigh with my aunt Katy."

"Starleigh?" The duke looked at her curiously. "Vincent Marlborough's estate?"

Cecelia stumbled against him, apologizing as he caught her arm. "Oh, excuse me. Yes, that was the owner's name I believe," she decreed, quickly recalling her error. "My aunt was, uh, employed on the estate for some years." Thank heavens she'd called Katherine Marlborough by her familial name of "Katy."

"Oh, I see," the duke nodded, having assumed such. "That was kind of the viscount to allow your relative to have you there."

Cecelia was relieved when further conversation was halted by the phalanx of young gentlemen descending upon them.

"Good morning, Miss Amber." Wally held the chair for Cecelia as Martha bustled about bringing her breakfast early the next day. "And congratulations on the play's success!"

"Why thank you, but how did you know it succeeded?" Cecelia laughed.

"I assumed, from those." The butler smiled, gesturing to the several arrangements about the small room. "And, there are more in the parlor. They've been arriving all morning."

"Oh, dear," Cecelia glanced about anxiously, "not more flowers?"

"I do not imagine you need be concerned about these, miss." The butler waylaid her fears. "From the varied cards, I expect they are strictly in tribute to your performance of last evening."

"There was no more jewelry?" she asked.

He chuckled. "No more diamonds, Miss Amber."

"Thank heavens." Cecelia laughed and excitedly began telling them of the play's outstanding success.

The Duke of Stanford was not having nearly so pleasant a morning, his own breakfast having been interrupted by a very smug Bexton.

"Philip?" The duke frowned up at his unwelcome early morning guest. "I cannot imagine what might have gotten you out of your bed before noon? Surely, you did not come to plague me with further remonstrations on Amber?"

"Not at all, my dear fellow." The lord casually peered at the assortment on Stanford's buffet and helped himself to a scone. "Actually, I have come to offer you my most humble apologies. I say—?" he gestured to the teapot.

Sighing, Julian called for his butler to fetch another cup. "Get on with it, Bexton. What are you really here for? I do not recall having asked for any apology on your ridiculous accusations that I stole the chit from you."

"Of course, you would be much too polite," the earl smoothly replied, relishing every moment of his revenge on the duke. "But, my dear friend, you should have! Why, I had no idea that you already had claims on the ladybird, or I should never have—"

"You knew very well that I was interested in Amber as I had that very morning in White's made the unfortunate mistake of alerting you to her existence."

"Oh yes, of course interested in. But Stanford, as we all know, in the muslin race it's the first to the sheets that counts! I thought the gel was still fair game. Had

I known you already had her in your keeping—'' he shrugged apologetically.

"What *are* you talking about?" Julian began to have an uneasy feeling. "I have not yet removed her from Levison's place, though I intend to do so shortly," he added with a warning glance.

Bexton artfully raised a brow. "Levison's place? Why my dear Julian, according to certain very reliable persons, that house is being paid for by none other than yourself."

With great effort, Bexton restrained his joy at the duke's expression.

"What?"

"You mean you didn't know that this protégé playwright of yours, has been charging all his mistress's expenses on your account?" Bexton laughed. "How droll. Here, all this time, you have been paying the blunt while Levison's enjoyed the benefits."

At the duke's expletive, Bexton cautiously decided it time to leave. "Well, I really must be going. I just thought perhaps you should want to know what your ladybird and her lover were about. Also you might want to check on your investment. I heard that Levison packed up and headed out of town a good deal before dawn this morning," he added with a grin.

Julian glared at the small stack of paid bills on his desk.

Barnstock, the duke's steward, had placed them there some days ago but with the play and recent estate problem Julian had not taken time to review them.

The duke's jaw tightened on finding Percival's signature on the let for Amber's house in with the batch of expenses Jamison, his solicitor, had paid for the playwright. He couldn't blame Jamison, as he had not advised the man what could be charged, merely given him a maximum amount to allow.

Julian flipped through the stack. It did appear as though the playwright had, at least, stayed well within the limits. But that was not now the point. Bexton, Stanford well knew, was doubtless already spreading the whole story through the ton. And, there was nothing a bored London society would delight in more than tittering over how the Duke of Stanford had been made to look the fool by a playwright and his mistress.

"Ayers!"

The ducal butler hurried in at his master's angry voice and in short order the duke's phaeton was readied and awaiting him at the mansion's front door.

"Y'er Grace." Beth, the young maid at the house where Percival resided, bobbed a nervous curtsy to Julian. "I'm sorry, Y'er Grace, but Mr. Levison had left out long a'for I comed in this morning. Oh, but he left a note for some 'un." she recalled as Julian started to turn away.

"Someone? For whom?"

"I don't rightly know, sir, as I don't read. I had planned to give it over to Mr. Simmons. He's the gentleman in the upper rooms to see if he couldn't have his man deliver it but—"

"Bring me the note, please." The duke stopped her anxious chattering in irritation.

The girl quickly scampered away to return with a thick packet.

Julian was surprised to find a note attached asking the chambermaid to have it delivered to himself first thing that morning.

Apparently, Levison hadn't realized the girl couldn't read.

"The letter is addressed to me." He handed the maid a coin in dismissal, opening it on the way back to his phaeton. Inside was a hastily scrawled message to himself as well as a second packet with Amber's name on it.

> Your Grace:
> Please forgive the informality of this note, but due to dire circumstances at my home in Cumbria, I'd no time to properly advise you of my departure. Please do not worry about the continuation of *Justine* in my absence as now the play is opened, the cast is quite capable of managing until I return.
> My only concern is that, I've had the evening's receipts delivered by strongbox to your solicitor, Mr. Jamison, after the performance last evening in accord with your previous instructions. As I'll not be able to return by the week's end to withdraw the cast's salary, I'd hoped perhaps you would authorize Jamison to release the necessary moneys to Miss Amber so that she may distribute them? Please be assured that you may trust her to take care of this matter.
> Also, if you'd be so kind, please have the enclosed letter delivered to her to explain my absence.
> I remain your most grateful servant,
>   Percival Levison.

The duke frowned. Dire circumstances? What dire circumstances? He considered the second sealed packet, obvious, from its thickness, containing a longer letter than his own.

The duke could think of no valid reason for the young man to have fled town. The play had been a resounding success. And, Levison had indeed had the funds from the box office sent to Jamison. The duke had checked with his solicitor immediately on discovering the playwright had left town in the middle of the night.

Despite the temptation, Julian decided he could not truly open the sealed missive of another, even a member of the muslin company. He would just personally deliver the letter to Amber and discover its content through her.

The duke tooled his phaeton skillfully through the narrow Hampstead streets, while he brooded over the matters Bexton had brought to light.

Levison certainly hadn't seemed the type to try to charge his mistress's keep on the ducal accounts. But then, the duke realized grimly, Levison didn't seem the type to even have a mistress in the first place.

But why hadn't the playwright even attempted to conceal the charges? Had he just assumed the duke, like many of the nobility, never deigned to check bills? And what of Amber? Had she known how the playwright was paying for her? The duke's countenance darkened ominously at that thought. Had the two of them been laughing at him behind his back all of this time?

Cecelia's smiling welcome to the duke vanished at his expression.

"Your Grace, is something amiss?" He had been so very charming last evening, she couldn't imagine what had happened.

"I must speak with you—alone," he added pointedly, glancing at her hovering abigail and butler, whose anxiously exchanged looks did nothing to allay his suspicions.

"Of course, Your Grace." Cecelia directed the duke

to the parlor. "Hannah, if you would please, bring a tea tray?" Cecelia asked, not wishing to be left alone with the duke in his apparent mood.

"Have you heard from Levison this morning?" the duke snapped as they entered the parlor.

"Percival?" Cecelia said in surprise. "No, but I do not expect to hear from him until this afternoon at the earliest, as I imagine he was out quite late last evening."

"You did not spend last night together?" Julian scarcely believed the young man would not have celebrated his success with his mistress, since much to his irritation, she had left the theater with Levison.

Cecelia blushed, unable to meet the duke's cool gaze. "No. Percival realized that I was quite tired last evening and merely brought me home."

Julian was in too ill of temper to be amused by her missish modesty. "So you are unaware that he has left town?"

"Left town?" Cecelia looked up in alarm. "Percy? Why ever would he—"

"He left a message for me that there was some dire emergency at his home and that he was leaving in the middle of the night."

"What emergency?" Cecelia anxiously moved to his side. "What did he say? Have you the message?"

Stanford drew the sealed letter from his coat pocket. "He did not advise me the nature of the problem. But perhaps he did in your letter?" He handed her the missive.

Cecelia turned away as she ripped open the envelope. "Oh, no!"

"What is it?" The duke turned her back to face him, and was surprised to find her eyes filling with tears.

"It is Constance." Cecelia impatiently dashed away

the tears blurring her vision as she tried to read the remainder of the letter.

Julian handed her a finely monogrammed handkerchief. "Constance?"

"Percy's wife. She is apparently—" Cecelia dabbed at her eyes.

"Here, would you like me to read it to you?" The duke impatiently reached for the papers but Cecelia moved quickly away.

"No. No, thank you." She scanned through the several sheets. "Constance is in her last stages of confinement with their child. It seems she has been suffering from some aguish fever." Cecelia read ahead anxiously. "Oh, merciful heavens!"

"What?" the duke prompted.

"Percy said Constance's physician is extremely concerned that they might lose the child," she managed not mentioning Percy's request that she watch over managing the play, nor his heartfelt entreaty at the end of the letter, that she pray for Constance and their baby.

The duke watched suspiciously when she read the remainder of the letter to herself. "He informed you of something else?"

"No, it is just personal things." Cecelia's evasive answer annoyed the duke even more.

"Indeed?" He gave her a cynical look. "Forgive me if I find it difficult to believe you are truly this distressed over your protector's wife and child!"

Already upset, Cecelia turned on him without thinking. "I do not care what you believe, Your Grace, but it happens that I love Percival! Of course, I care about his family! I should not wish anyone to lose a child, especially Constance"—her voice broke—"oh, I could not expect you, of all people, to understand!"

The duke was more taken aback by her avowed love

for the playwright, than her daring to speak to him in such a way.

As he remained distantly silent, Cecelia realized she had scarcely treated him as an actress should one of the highest members of the peerage.

"I apologize, Your Grace. That was unseemly of me."

The duke accepted the apology coolly. "You have had an unsettling experience. However, this degree of attraction you seem to have developed for Levison, does concern me." He led her to the sofa and seated himself beside her.

"I am afraid I do not understand?" Cecelia had not expected that to be his complaint.

The duke started to speak but stopped when Hannah entered with the tea tray. While the abigail fussed about the table, Julian considered his options.

Since this Levison had left the scene there was no longer an obstacle to him taking Amber under his own protection, if he yet decided to proceed on that course. In fact, the duke acknowledged wryly, he would not now even be obliged to remove her from this house first, since he was apparently already fronting the blunt for it!

Finally noticing the abigail was taking much too long arranging the tea table, Julian looked over impatiently. "I am certain your mistress can finish that. You may be excused."

Much to the duke's growing ire, Hannah glanced at Cecelia for permission. "My la—uh Miss Amber?"

"It's all right Hannah, you may go," Cecelia nodded rather absently. What on earth had the duke so upset then if it wasn't the moneys—unless—he discovered their subterfuge!

"And close the door!"

Cecelia started guiltily at Julian's curt order.

"Do you take cream, Your Grace?" Cecelia reached for the teapot to delay the coming confrontation, but the duke had been put off far too long.

"I did not come here for tea. I came here for answers," he snapped.

Cecelia carefully controlled her expression as she replaced the teapot on the tray. "Yes?"

"Are you aware of who is paying the let on your house?" He decided to come right to the point.

Cecelia blinked. "What house?"

"This one, of course."

"Why—Percival is," Cecelia stammered.

"And where is Levison getting the funds for your expenses?"

"What do you mean, where is he getting them?" Cecelia asked in confusion. Why should the duke be so concerned where Percival got money to support her? Cecelia looked up in alarm. "Surely, you are not imagining that Percy is engaged in some illegal activities or something and that is why you think he left town?"

Julian paused. "I cannot actually say Levison had any illegal intention, however, I can scarcely credit he imagined I would sanction the use of my funds to pay your expenses."

"What do you mean your funds?" Cecelia asked before suddenly understanding. "Oh no! You are not saying Percival used your advances to pay for this house?" She stared at him aghast.

"Yes. It appears I have been providing for your support all along," Julian countered dryly.

"Good heavens. This is all my fault!" In her distress Cecelia missed the duke's cynical meaning. "I should have known Percy did not have the funds on his own and I insisted that he provide me a residence!"

"I believe that is generally expected in these arrangements," Julian muttered darkly, but Cecelia ignored it.

"Your Grace, Percival is honest, almost to a fault! I assure you he has every intention of paying you back. He would never—"

"I am not concerned over the moneys." The duke cut her off, further irritated by her championing the playwright. "His advances were guaranteed by the play's receipts. And, as Levison did not attempt to disguise what he was doing with the funds, I can only assume he intended no fraud."

Cecelia stared at him in confusion. "Then why are you so angry?"

The duke was silent a moment. It was quite galling to have the ton twittering about the incident behind his back, but Julian knew no one would dare confront him openly, and the matter would soon be forgotten. His greater irritation he realized was on Amber's account. He had been quite looking forward to their relationship—and now?

"You are angry at me?" Cecelia guessed at the duke's expression. Had he then really found out about her and Percy? She suddenly recalled his remark on being concerned about her feelings for Percival. Had he said that as a hint that he knew about them?

"Is it my relationship with Percival?" she forced herself to ask.

The duke smiled wryly. "I know it should not matter. In fact, I cannot say why it annoyed me so much for you to say you loved the man."

"I—"

Julian looked down at the confusion in the lovely eyes meeting his so anxiously, and his own gaze softened. "No, that was not the truth," he admitted, raising one hand to gently stroke down her cheek. "I was not just annoyed, I was jealous because you were speaking of Levison instead of me.''

"Your Grace?" Cecelia's eyes were filled with wonder at something sweet and warm that seemed to bloom within her at his touch—his words.

The duke drew in his breath at the look in her eyes, forgetting all but an aching need. "My name is Julian, my love," he corrected, his lips lowering to hers.

"Julian." Forgetting who the duke thought she was, Cecelia murmured his name against his lips, her arms sliding about the duke's neck quite naturally as he drew her to him.

"Ah, my darling," the duke murmured huskily some moments later on finally releasing her lips. "You can not know how I have longed to do that."

Cecelia lips curved in a soft smile as she looked up at him and with a groan the duke bent to again kiss the corners of her mouth before trailing more kisses down her throat. "You are enough to drive a man mad, my beloved, I do not know that I can wait until tonight."

"Tonight?" Cecelia asked vaguely, but the duke's lips again raised to hers and she forgot her question.

It was only when she felt the duke's hand move from her waist unerringly upward that Cecelia stiffened in shock.

"Julian?" Her own hand closed over his, stopping him.

The duke frowned momentarily, but then chuckled, moving slightly away. "Forgive me, my sweet. You are right." Raising her hand to his lips, he kissed her fingers. "I suppose that bloody abigail is likely to come back at any moment. But as Levison is gone, you shain't mind my coming back here tonight, will you?"

Cecelia stared up at him, finally understanding. And she had thought he actually—!

"Amber?" The duke tried to draw her back to him but she struggled away.

"No, please don't." She turned her lips from his, wanting to scream. To cry. All the sweet emotions within her curled into an intense pain as she realized what he had intended—what he wanted from her.

"Amber, what is the matter?" The duke turned her back to him in concern.

"I am sorry—I—I cannot—do that."

The duke abruptly released her. "Cannot? Because of this love you have just discovered for Levison, I assume?" he snapped in frustration at her responding to him so delightfully one moment and pushing him away the next.

"No, Julian, please, I—" she placed a hand on his arm to stop him as he went to rise. She could not remain in this role anymore. She had to tell him—and hope he would understand.

The duke glanced down at her hand pointedly. "Now it is 'please, Julian'? I see. Perhaps I was too precipitous. Should I have discussed the financial arrangements first?" he suggested curtly.

Cecelia paled. Removing her hand from the duke's arm, she carefully began again. "Your Grace, I am trying to explain, Percival and I are—"

"Damn it, Amber!" The duke stood in unreasoning fury. "I am in no mood to hear you plead your love for your playwright. In fact, at the moment it would take very little to convince me to throw Levison and his whole bloody troupe out of my theater—including you—so I would be extremely careful what I say, were I you!"

Avoiding Cecelia's shocked look, the duke strode across the room to stare out the window in frustration. He knew his anger at the unassuming playwright was quite out of proportion to the situation. The woman was after all, but a cyprian. What on earth had come over him?

Cecelia stared at the duke's back in horror. Dear heaven, what had she done? Percival had always said her foolish ideas would get her into real trouble one day! But she could never have imagined the possibility of this hurting so many people! If he closed the play . . .

Cecelia knew she didn't dare tell the duke the truth now. And she couldn't leave, not now, after all they had done to make the play a success. But she couldn't stay here in this house, not with him paying for it.

She had to move, though she had no idea what she'd use for funds. What little jewelry she had inherited had long since been sold to support the estate and the floods last spring had set her back a whole year on the property's small income. It would be a terrible risk, but they could move to Somersett House here in London, though that yet would require moneys she did not have, to run it.

"Your Grace, I will move from here, if you wish."

The duke gave a mirthless laugh, "Move? Move where? Your Percival cannot even afford this place! Or perhaps you can support yourself on an actress's salary?"

Cecelia raised her chin. "We shall manage. It need not be your concern."

"Not my concern?" the duke repeated, his tone dangerously quiet. "Have you any idea how much your playwright has charged on my accounts?"

"No, but you said that was to be repaid by the play?"

"Precisely," Julian snapped. "The play is collateral for his loans. And without you, my dear, there would be no play. So you can see, I have a very valid concern about where you are and what you are doing."

"I have no intention of abandoning the play," Cecelia said softly.

The duke looked at her silently a moment. "You may remain here for the time being," he advised curtly. "However," he added with a cold look, "while you are living in this house, it would be wise to remember who is paying your bills. I will not put up with your entertaining any other males here, including Levison, from now on."

He might as well have slapped her, from the shock on her face.

The duke placed his hand on her shoulder stopping her, as she silently turned away. He could not let her leave like that. "Wait, Amber. That was quite unfair of me. You had no way of knowing it was my funds paying for the house and nor do I truly suspect you would welcome any males—other than your Percival." He paused. "But your love for the man is quite hopeless, my dear, you must see that?" The duke was surprised at the pain he felt when she finally looked up at him, her eyes glistening with unshed tears.

"I know—"

The duke had no way of knowing her simple acknowledgment did not refer to the playwright. He raised a hand, lean fingers stroking down her cheek before gently raising her chin. "Forget your playwright, my sweet"—he murmured, his lips but lightly brushing hers—"and I promise—I shall make his loss up to you."

Cecelia stood very still for several long minutes after the duke left.

Chapter Eight

"Dear heaven, Miss Cecelia!" Hannah gasped later, when her mistress told her a carefully edited rendition of the morning's happenings.

"Poor Mr. Levison! I do hope Mrs. Levison and the child will be all right."

"As do I," Cecelia sighed. "I wish there were some way of knowing, but I suppose we'll have to wait for a letter."

"And I can hardly believe that duke!" the abigail sniffed. "I feared something of this nature when I saw the way he kept looking at you. And, Mr. Wordsworth well knew what was brewing. That definitely puts paid to your staying here." She turned determinedly to the nearest wardrobe. "I shall begin our packing."

"No, Hannah." Cecelia stopped her. "I cannot leave."

"What?" Her abigail turned to her in disbelief. "After the man so much as demanded you be his *mistress!*"

Cecelia carefully looked away. "It was an understandable assumption. After all, His Grace merely believes what we have presented for him to believe.'' Not wishing to cause the staff more concern, she merely said the duke was allowing them to remain in the house, not saying for how long.

"But you cannot stay here!" Hannah stared at her in alarm. "Miss Cecelia, that man has already compromised you—in there alone in the parlor—and him a gentleman—even thinking such as that!"

"Hannah," Cecelia soothed her abigail, "you forget that the woman the duke had in the parlor was Amber, an actress. In all honesty, on thinking back to previous conversations with the duke, I fear I have been quite naive. In fact, I suspect I have doubtless led him to believe I would be agreeable to his suggestion."

"Miss Cecelia!"

"Now please don't go missish on me," Cecelia sighed. "There are only two weeks until the play's end, I am sure I can distract the duke until then."

"Distract?"

"Stanford truly is a gentleman. He would never force a lady—or even an actress to—to his will."

Hannah shook her head in distress. "I fear this is all a great mistake Miss Cecelia. Mr. Levison would never want you to put yourself in such danger for his play."

"Percival must never learn of this," Cecelia said firmly. "You know how he is. He would be incensed with the duke and probably walk out without any regard to his future."

"As well he should," the abigail muttered.

"Hannah, you will give me your word, that you won't say anything?"

"I suppose," the woman agreed reluctantly.

"Now, I must prepare for this evening's performance," Cecelia changed the subject. "As Percy's taken the carriage, I suppose I shall have to have a hackney. Could you tell Wally to see about acquiring one? And ask Mrs. Cochran to send up bath water?"

It turned out, however, that much to the abigail's alarm, a hired carriage was unnecessary.

"I am Barnstock, the Duke of Stanford's steward."

An impeccable young man was politely introducing himself to the butler when Hannah came back downstairs later to be sure the hackney had arrived.

"His Grace has sent a carriage for your mistress's disposal. He assumed she might need one, as Mr. Levison has departed with theirs."

"That was quite kind of His Grace." The butler's anxious glance brought Hannah over. "His Grace has provided Miss Amber a carriage."

"How thoughtful." Hannah glanced out in dismay at the handsome brougham, emblazoned with the ducal seal. "But what are those servants unloading?"

"His Grace has also sent provisions with word that he will be dining here after the evening's performance," Barnstock continued blandly. "If you could advise me where to direct the servants to take them?"

"Uh, the kitchen is off the west entrance," Hannah said distractedly. "But surely those crates are not all food for this evening?"

The steward restrained a smile. "No. His Grace also directed we restock your pantries for future visits. And, of course, he has sent his own plate and napery."

"Of course." The abigail and butler exchanged a glance.

"Whatever is going on?" Cecelia came down the stairs.

"The duke sent his steward, Miss Amber," Wally advised.

Barnstock smiled to himself as Cecelia approached. By heaven, Stanford had done well for himself! This one looked amazingly refined and lovely beyond words.

"His Grace has advised that if there is anything you wish, Miss Amber, you need only ask," the duke's steward advised.

With effort, Cecelia contained her composure. "Please express my appreciation to the duke, but I am sure there is nothing more I shall need."

"Miss—" both Hannah and Wally began the second Barnstock left but Cecelia was in no state to listen to their concerns.

"I know. I know," she waved them both away, "but I assure you it will be all right. Now, I really have to leave for the theater."

Cecelia was appalled to find the whole cast of *Justine* outside the Barcelly Theatre, spending the last few minutes in the cool of the huge oaks before entering to prepare for the evening's performance.

They had taken little notice of the duke's carriage but stared in surprise when his footman handed her from the brougham rather than Stanford as they had expected.

"Now fancy that!" Vivian teased good-naturedly when Cecelia came over. "Our playwright has been gone but a day and here you are already comfortably ensconced in the duke's carriage. I don't blame you, sweetie." The actress grinned at Cecelia's flushed face. "I knew you'd come to your senses sooner or later."

"Really I didn't—I wouldn't—I mean, Percival," Cecelia stammered in embarrassment at the grins of her fellow actors.

"Don't let Viv get to you." Daniel came over to give

her a light hug. "Stanford seems to be a pretty good cove. And, with Levison running off back to his wife like that." He shrugged.

"You do not understand, Percy's wife is pregnant and he had to leave."

"Amber, you really don't have to explain," Vivian laughed. "Percival is really nice and a great playwright but"—she winked."—a duke? None of us blame you, do we girls?"

"See?" She grinned when the other female members of the cast expressed enthusiastic support.

"Come on," Daniel chuckled with the rest. "Let the lady be and let's do get on with the play."

Cecelia was a little shocked at the ease with which the group accepted her presumed switch of protectors. However with their lack of censure she decided it more practicable to let them think as they wished, especially since she doubted she could change their opinion anyway.

Much as Percival had expected, the cast managed fine without him and the first act of *Justine* received a standing ovation when the curtains closed for intermission.

"It looks as if your duke is going to watch every performance!" Daniel chuckled, nodding up at the duke as he walked by.

Cecelia had carefully avoided even looking toward the private boxes during the play, but now glanced up at Daniel's direction. Unfortunately, Julian had just turned to greet an elegant lady entering his box.

Vivian caught Cecelia's expression as the duke raised the ravishing woman's hand to his lips.

"Do not be upset, love. That is the Countess of Vierant," the actress said sympathetically. "She was a past amore of your duke and he is renown for never taking a woman back once he's through with her. Besides, as quick as your duke has taken you over from Mr. Levison, I doubt he's going to be looking out for a bride any time soon," she laughed, obviously thinking that should make the other actress feel better.

"Come on, Nelly's waiting to change your gown for the next act."

The highlight of the final act was Justine's lament decrying her impossible love for the seaman and Cecelia found her present mood in perfect accord with the role. Her sweet voice wafting Percival's soulful lines over the audience, soon had the ladies, both young and old, groping for their handkerchiefs.

Julian even found himself moved by the poignant scene. She was an astonishingly good actress as well as singer. The duke's pleasure in watching Cecelia however vanished as Justine turned toward the audience, her cheeks glistening with tears.

The duke's eyes darkened. Was it but theater tears Amber wept, for Justine's lover, or real tears—for her own?

When they finally finished the last curtain call, Cecelia headed for her small dressing room in relief.

Vivian parted the curtains dividing the dressing rooms just as Nelly lifted the last act's expensive gown carefully over Cecelia's head.

"We're all going to The Gryphon and Unicorn for a late supper. Want to join us, Amber? Oops, I guess not. Sorry, Your Grace," Vivian chuckled, dropping the curtain back in place.

"What?" Cecelia's voice was muffled beneath the yards of material, as the costume girl quickly slipped the dress the rest of the way off.

"Nelly!" Cecelia protested but the girl merely giggled, and left the room, taking the gown with her.

Cecelia turned in expectant horror to find the Duke of Stanford's eyes wandering over her thin chemise with undisguised appreciation. She glanced frantically about for her robe only to have him pull it from a hook on the door beside him.

"I expect this is what you are looking for?" Julian smiled laconically as he brought it over. "Though it is a crime to cover up such loveliness." He draped the garment over her shoulders, staying to lift her tangled locks outside the robe as she grasped the front edges anxiously together.

The duke's hands moved from her hair to rest invitingly on her shoulders but Cecelia carefully did not look up.

"Thank you, Your Grace." She forced herself to step away from his touch.

The duke turned curtly away to give her privacy. "You may proceed with your dressing. Have you Levison's forwarding address?"

"Yes. Did you need to contact him?" Cecelia glanced at the duke anxiously over her shoulder as she slipped into the simple gown she'd worn to the theater.

"No. Another letter arrived for him, apparently after his departure his landlord had it sent to me."

"Another letter, from whom?" She came back over beside him, while yet struggling with the last buttons up the back of the gown.

"There was no return." Unasked, he turned her around to finish the buttoning.

"Thank you." She smiled tentatively. "Have you the letter now?"

Without comment, the duke brought an envelope from his coat pocket and handed it to her.

Cecelia easily recognized the graceful hand. "Oh, it

is from Constance. Percy would not mind my reading it."

The duke's brows drew together in perplexity as Cecelia ripped open the letter from Percival's wife.

"Oh, Julian!" Cecelia smiled in relief as she scanned through the missive, not even realizing she had used the duke's Christian name. "Constance's fever broke the day after her mother sent the other letter."

Without thinking, Cecelia began reading aloud. "The physician insists that I remain in bed to ward against the fever's return, but he is confident the most serious part of malaise is past. But I pray you might yet come home to me, Percival, as there is still some concern that the fever could have caused harm to our child and I could not bear to be without you if—" Cecelia stopped and folded the letter. "Oh, the poor dear. I hope Percival has reached her! I fear I know so little about the medical field." Cecelia looked up at the duke hopefully. "Surely, her fever should not really affect the baby, do you think?"

"It does not seem likely, though I must confess to little knowledge in that area myself," Julian answered rather bemused at the entire conversation. "Come now, I expect your cook should have dinner waiting." He started to escort her out, but Cecelia stopped him.

"I am afraid I shall need another few moments."

The duke smiled as she gestured to her stockings and slippers yet sitting on a nearby stool.

"Oh. Very well, I will await you by my carriage outside."

Chapter Nine

The duke lit a cheroot thoughtfully as he waited under the huge sprawling oak tree for Cecelia to finish dressing.

He had never in his experience with the demimonde run across a woman like Amber. She was not only lovely and talented but gracious in manner, caring, intelligent. In fact, Julian acknowledged, she held all the qualities any man could ask for, except of course, that she was another man's mistress.

Oddly depressed by his thoughts, Julian extinguished his cigar and leaned against the oak watching moodily as a light breeze rustled the dark branches about him.

" 'T'is sweet to listen as the night winds creep from leaf to leaf.' "

The duke turned to find Cecelia had come up unnoticed.

"*Don Juan?*" He smiled, barely repressing an almost instinctive desire to take her in his arms as she leaned on the tree beside him.

"Mm. So beautifully tragic, was it not?"

"Lord Byron's element," Julian agreed. "A bit like parts of *Justine*. You had half the audience in tears with the tragic beauty of Justine's lost love in the third act. It appeared you even wept yourself. Real tears, for a fictional love?" he asked idly, "Or, for your real love?"

Cecelia looked up at the duke, startled. He couldn't know, could he?

"Never mind." Julian turned brusquely to the carriage. "I expect we are making your cook quite anxious trying to keep dinner warm."

"You have seen the play so many times, with rehearsals and all. I should think you would find it tedious by now," Cecelia commented mainly for conversation, as the carriage rumbled over the cobbled road.

"I could never find listening to you sing tedious." The duke glanced down at her. "Nor watching you, for that matter."

Cecelia could think of no reply to that and the remainder of the trip was in silence.

"Good evening, Your Grace. Miss Amber."

"Good evening, Wally." Cecelia smiled but Julian gave the butler a hard glance at something in the man's manner.

That rather bizarre housekeeper Amber had found was always friendly enough, but the butler and that hovering abigail had become increasingly cool in their attitude toward him. You should think that they would be eager for their mistress to obtain a more prosperous protector than that miserly playwright, since it would obviously benefit their own lot as well.

"Shall I have dinner served now?" Wally addressed

the question staidly to a neutral point somewhere between the two of them.

"Yes, thank you, Wally. I am quite famished." Cecelia smiled before catching the duke's raised brow. "If, of course, that pleases Your Grace?" she offered belatedly, as it seemed they had at least temporarily, called a truce.

Julian nodded with a cool look at the butler. "You may serve the Stanford burgundy with dinner."

"You have your own winery?" Cecelia asked as he escorted her into the dining room.

"I did have—once. An unfortunate investment in France, before this most recent unpleasantness."

Cecelia stared at the delicate cut crystal, gold rimmed plate and snowy embossed linen on her table.

"Really Your Grace, it was not necessary that you should—" she began in concern but he cut her off.

"It is nothing," he dismissed, naturally moving to the head of the table, "and I believe you called me Julian before?"

Cecelia flushed as her thoughts flew, not to her reading of Constance's letter to which the duke referred, but rather to the previous evening in his arms.

Julian's lips quirked. He easily guessed the reason for her blush, but graciously did not comment on it.

"You may pour the wine, Wordsworth," he nodded to the waiting butler. "You shall appreciate this burgundy, my dear, though it is of recent vintage."

Cecelia returned to his earlier remark. "You couched ownership of the winery in the past tense?"

"I had to withdraw my overseer due to Bonaparte's ambitions," Julian explained, "so I rather expect the property has been taken by the populace. Though but a small investment, I cannot be pleased at its loss, as it consistently produced an exceptional grape."

Cecelia sipped the heady wine in approval. "This is

quite excellent. Apparently, you were able to save some of your stock before the borders closed.''

"I managed to save the bottled wine and even brought cuttings from the vineyard which are now growing at Stanford.''

"Do the vines yet thrive here?''

"Too abundantly in fact,'' the duke grimaced. "They have quite taken over my arbor. But they now bear a grape so sweet as to be worthless for naught but the making of jellies for a village fair.''

Cecelia laughed. "Perhaps I might beg a few cuttings from you. I could use a sweet grape for my conserve.''

Julian raised a brow in amusement. "Conserve? Marmalade too, no doubt. My dear Amber, have your talents no end?''

In good nature, Cecelia joined with his teasing. "Sir,'' she declared archly, "you would not make light of my sweets, had you tried them.''

Cecelia stared uncomprehending as the duke almost choked in laughter. "I assure you, my dear, that is a pleasure I await with great anticipation.''

Finally realizing her *faux pas* Cecelia couldn't restrain a giggle, "Julian, you know very well that's not what I meant!''

"No?'' The duke grinned. "A pity. I had hoped it preluded an invitation.''

"You are abominable,'' she sniffed, attempting to regain some decorum as Mrs. Cochran came in with the first course.

Julian was surprised at his own enjoyment of Amber's company. She was a delightful conversationalist and seemed in quite good humor, which was puzzling. One would have thought she should have shown some distress at being denied her lover's presence. Or could that whole display of love for her Percival have been a delay. Perhaps she expected to obtain a better offer from him by keeping him waiting?

The duke frowned at his thoughts. He should doubtless just leave Amber to her playwright. There were plenty of equally lovely, and much more obliging females in London. But there was something about this one, from which Julian could not make himself walk away.

"Would you care to have your port brought to the parlor, Your Grace?" Wally made the standard offer reluctantly as he feared the duke would closet himself alone with Miss Amber again.

"Yes, and you may bring in the sherry I had sent over, for your mistress."

Cecelia found herself becoming again nervous about the duke's intentions, as he led her into the parlour, though he had previously advised her that he was only coming to dine.

"That will be all, Wordsworth. I shall pour." The duke dismissed the butler, following behind him to close the door.

"I merely wish to speak to you in private," he advised Cecelia at her anxious glance.

He filled their glasses and brought them to the settee before the fireplace.

"Kindly sit down, Amber," he said impatiently, handing her a glass of sherry.

"Thank you."

The duke took a nearby chair. "It did not appear you found dining with me too trying?" He took a sip from his port, watching her.

"I am sure you are aware that I enjoy your company— usually," Cecelia allowed carefully, not knowing his point.

Julian smiled. "And I, yours—usually. That being the

case, do you not think we can come to some—arrangement?''

"Your Grace, I have explained—''

"Come now, my dear,'' the duke interrupted. "Is your reticence truly from your feelings for Levison? Or are there other factors involved?''

"Other factors?'' Cecelia managed, carefully not looking at him. "I don't know what ever you could mean?''

The duke sighed. "Amber, let's not play games. I can be a very generous man when I desire something, and I should think it rather obvious that I want you. You may name your price.''

"You think that I wish money!'' Cecelia gasped.

The duke gave a wry laugh. "That is the usual arrangement, I believe.''

Cecelia sat her glass down and rose in distress. "If you will excuse me.''

Julian was oddly relieved that he had been wrong. "No, I will not excuse you. Sit down, Amber,'' he said firmly, himself standing as she reluctantly resumed her seat.

The duke restlessly paced across the small room.

"Then you really do care for Levison?'' he finally asked, coming back before her.

"Yes.''

He looked at her a moment. "And what shall you do when this season is finished? Frankly, Levison seems more the family man. Do you truly believe he would take a mistress back to Cumbria where his wife and new child await?''

"Well—I—'' Cecelia stammered, unable to even voice such a lie about her cousin.

"Of course he would not. You know that, as well as I,'' Julian offered more gently.

When Cecelia remained silent, the duke continued.

"I've decided to continue paying your expenses here, at least for the play's duration." He waved aside her attempt to speak. "Amber, I am not a very patient man but I shall attempt to understand these feeling you have for your playwright, and not expect more of you, than your company, for the time being. And when the play has adjourned, you may have the choice of changing your decision—or leaving. Is that agreeable?"

Though it seemed a perfect solution to her problems, Cecelia hesitated guiltily. "Your Grace, though your offer is quite generous, I must advise you that my answer shall be the same then as now."

"That is one chance I am willing to take." The duke smiled confidently, remembering her response to his kisses.

Chapter Ten

As the week progressed, Cecelia found herself quite looking forward to the duke's company at the end of each day.

He had been present for at least part of both matinee and evening performances of *Justine* every day since their discussion and always awaited her in her dressing room after the last act. Though he had twice taken her to dinner at his own home, the duke had made no attempt to further their relationship. In fact, he scarcely touched her but for a chaste kiss at each evening's end, which, if the truth were known, Cecelia was beginning to find extremely frustrating.

Thursday however, the duke's box remained empty and Julian's coach arrived that evening with none but the footman to escort her.

"You are home early tonight, Miss Amber," Wally greeted her as he took her wrap.

"Yes. I don't suppose the duke mentioned coming to dinner?" she casually asked.

"No, miss. But you received a message from him earlier." Wally handed her a missive bearing the ducal seal.

Cecelia took it eagerly into the parlor. "My dear Amber," the note stated in Julian's firm hand. "Matters on my estate have necessitated my presence, so I fear I must deprive myself of your company this evening. As I am not certain how long I may be in the country, I have arranged that my steward, Barnstock, shall be on hand should there be anything you need or any problems arise with the play."

Cecelia smiled wryly on reading that he had advised Barnstock to deliver and disburse the moneys for the cast salaries Friday, ignoring what she knew was Percival's advice that she might handle the task.

The brief message ended with Julian's intention to return early the next week and was signed formally, Stanford.

"Is there a problem, miss?" Wally questioned at his mistress's drawn brow.

"No." Cecelia tried to keep the disappointment from her voice. "The duke was only advising me he has been called to his country estate, so you and Hannah can cease worrying, for the next few days at least."

The old butler actually flushed. "Miss Amber, we are only concerned for your welfare."

"I know. And I do appreciate your concern, but the duke has been nothing but a gentleman these last few days. I am quite sure you are worrying for naught."

"Of course, miss," Wally agreed, though hearing Cecelia sigh as she wandered off rereading Stanford's note, his concern for his mistress but deepened.

When Saturday evening brought no further word from either Percival or the duke, Cecelia found herself in a morass of megrims. Since Barcelly Theater was

LADY CECELIA'S CHARADE   111

closed on the Sabbath, she decided to request the duke's carriage to drive into the country.

"It will be pleasant to retreat from the bustle and noise of town," she told Hannah. "We shall have Martha pack us a picnic and find some pleasant spot to while away the day."

Hannah, unbeknownst to her mistress, had been carrying on a flirtation with the duke's burly coachman, and was quite willing to fall in with any plan that included Alvin's company. "What a splendid idea! I shall help Martha with the luncheon."

To Cecelia's pleasure, the summer day dawned quite clear and warm.

Assuming they would see no one, Cecelia chose to wear one of her favorite gowns, a garden dress in sprigged muslin, embroidered delicately with trailing roses. She had not worn that particular gown since coming to London, deeming it too ladylike for Amber, but decided it might help lift her spirits.

Cecelia also refused to allow Hannah to apply Amber's usual make-up, stating the fresh air would be good for her complexion, though the truth was, the whole role of the actress had become quite depressing.

"Where may we take you, Miss Amber?" the duke's coachman inquired politely, directing the postilion and the footman to load the various hampers onto the carriage.

"I am not overly familiar with the area," Cecelia admitted. "Might you suggest somewhere? We had hoped to find a pretty spot out in the country, perhaps with a lake or stream to lay our picnic beside."

"Well," the coachman considered. "There is a nice field only a bit south of town we often pass on the way to Stanford. As it belongs to the duke, there would be no one to complain of you using it, and as I recall, it has a pleasant little copse of trees beside a stream."

"That sounds perfect." Cecelia allowed the footman to hand her into the duke's plush traveling coach. "Is it very far?" she asked, turning just in time to catch Alvin giving Hannah a bold wink.

"Oh uh, no, miss." The coachman straightened instantly. "It's but half hour's ride at most."

"And just what was that wink all about?" Cecelia teased her abigail once the coach lumbered onto the roadway.

"Wink?" Hannah grinned. "Oh you must have thought that the coachman—heavens, my lady, the poor man but had a cinder in his eye."

"A cinder? My, now that can be quite painful. Perhaps when we stop you should see if you can help him get it out?" Cecelia laughed.

"How thoughtful of you, my lady." Hannah giggled. "I might offer to help, if you don't require my company."

The field, much as Alvin had promised, was delightful—an emerald gem sloping down to a crystal stream and tall graceful willows.

The coachman managed to find a narrow break in the hedgerow to drive the brougham through, though he dared not take the heavy equipage too far into the field.

In scarcely any time, the servants had the carriage unloaded and the picnic laid out on blankets by the stream's bank. They then retreated discretely to have their own lunch under an oak, close enough to watch over both the women and the carriage.

Cecelia sighed in pleasure as she settled herself on

the sun-dappled blanket. "I hadn't realized how much I miss the country." She untied the ribbons of her bonnet and removed it, allowing the light breeze to tease with her hair as it wished.

Hannah glanced at her mistress as she set out a selection of collations from the filled hampers. "My lady, you must admit you've enjoyed all the activity of London. I quite expect you're going to miss it, when you return to Somersett."

Cecelia was rather surprised at her own dismay on the thought of returning to her estate. She had previously enjoyed her independence, but now it somehow seemed lonely. "Yes, I expect you are correct," she answered lightly. "I shall miss it—or at least some of it."

"Such as being the star of Justine," Hannah grinned. "Adored by all those silly young lords?"

"Playing Justine has been an adventure." Cecelia smiled, though knowing that was not at all what she would miss.

After finishing their luncheon Cecelia brought out a novel she had begun some time before. "I do believe I see your coachman over there worrying with that cinder," she lazily advised Hannah as she leaned back against a tree to read.

"My heavens, so he is." Hannah laughed, as the coachman smiled toward her hopefully.

As the peace of the warm, summer afternoon settled about her, Cecelia soon laid her book aside.

After stopping midway back to London for the noon meal, the duke had decided to send his carriage on ahead. He had purchased a handsome young gelding while in the country and determined to enjoy the pleasant weather by riding the remainder of the way.

Julian unfortunately discovered that the roan had an unpleasant gait too late to catch up with his coach and by the time he passed the final turn-stile to London, his mood was brooding toward murderous.

"Bloody son of Satan!" Julian shifted uncomfortably in the saddle as his mount loped down the carriageway, but at least he was nearing a parcel of his own land which had a pleasant stream. Perhaps he could stop there for at least a few minutes respite.

The duke topped the hill in anticipation only to find a large coach pulled off the carriageway just where he had intended going.

"Blasted poachers doubtless fishing in my trout stream again!" Julian muttered irritably, but as he closed on the vehicle, his frown faded.

The coach was none other than his own, and surely that was Amber's abigail with his coachman? Hopefully scanning the area, the duke smiled on espying the blanket graced by a distinctively female form next to his stream. Ignoring the roan's painful stride, the duke urged his mount forward.

"Your Grace!" Alvin abruptly released Hannah as his master quite unexpectedly rode up. "We were just, that is—Miss Amber wished to—"

The duke found himself in suddenly too good of a humor to spoil the man's *tete-a-tete*.

"Cut line, Alvin. I cannot say when the sight of my own coach has been more welcome." Leaping down, Julian tossed his horse's reins to the coachman. "You may have this bloody beast delivered to Tattersal's for their next auction."

Alvin grinned, giving the leggy roan a considering glance. "Hm. Withers are a bit high. I'd expect he has a mighty rough gait."

The duke gave the man a lowering glance. "Where

in blue blazes were you when I bought the animal?'' He glanced back over toward the stream. "That is Amber, I expect?''

"Yes, sir. But she may be sleeping,'' Hannah advised. "Shall I awake her?''

"No, I will,'' he said, rather to the abigail's concern. "You may continue your conversation with Alvin.''

The duke smiled as he looked down at the sleeping woman. She appeared different today somehow—so young and innocent in sleep—one would scarcely know her not to be a lady.

His expression stilling on his thoughts, the duke sat down beside Cecelia. "Amber?'' Brushing a tendril of red gold from her forehead Julian allowed his fingers to continue down the soft curve of her cheek.

Cecelia sighed as her quite pleasant dreams began to merge with reality at the duke's touch.

"Are you awake, my sweet?'' The duke leaned over her.

Cecelia opened her eyes and smiled, though yet half asleep as the duke's lips brushed hers in a gentle caress.

"Julian?'' Cecelia blinked not quite sure if the kiss had been real or merely a part of her dream. "What are you doing here?''

Julian laughed softly. "Enjoying a quite delightful surprise.'' His gaze moved over the sweetness of her sleep flushed face, but since the servants were yet in sight, he stifled the desire to take her in his arms. "Did you have a pleasant picnic?''

"Oh yes, it is so lovely here and much cooler than in town. You were on your way back to London?'' she asked hopefully.

"Yes. My estate was having some problems with flooding but the worst is over now. Come.'' He stood and offered her his hand. "Why don't we walk? This stream forms a pretty waterfall down that hill over there, I should like to show you.''

''Really?'' Cecelia took his hand and rose gracefully. ''Oh dear. I quite forgot I had removed my slippers.'' She glanced indecisively to where her stockings and slippers had long since been discarded in an untidy heap.

Julian chuckled, scarcely having missed the delightful bare feet and ankles as he came up. ''You shan't need them. If we come upon any briars I will carry you.''

''You had best hope the way is clear then,'' Cecelia teased, allowing her hand to remain quite naturally in his, ''as I have doubtless put on a stone in weight, from all the sweets Martha packed in our hamper.''

''If you have, it is naught but becoming.'' The duke's gaze moving appreciatively over her. ''Might I say, you look especially lovely this afternoon.''

''Thank you,'' Cecelia blushed, changing the subject. ''Alvin said this land belongs to you. Do you come here often?''

''Not lately, but when a lad I caught many a trout in this stream. In fact,'' he indicated a large flat stone on the opposite bank, ''if I correctly recall, I cooked my very last catch over an open fire on that rock.''

''You cook?'' Cecelia looked up at him in disbelief.

The duke raised a brow. ''Of course. No doubt you are one of those who assume nobles incapable of anything productive?''

''Well,'' Cecelia grinned, ''I admit I have been known to espouse that opinion, but more recently, I have found not all nobles to be the same.'' Her eye was caught by a slight riffle in a shallow pool of the stream. ''Oh, look, there is one of your trout now, tailing for nymphs, it is not?''

''Mm.'' The duke barely glanced at the silver flutter

as he worried over her statement. Not realizing her jest on nobles was aimed at him, Julian found her reference to other males quite annoying, though he had never even considered his previous mistresses' pasts.

"You have known very many noblemen?" he asked casually.

"More than I might have wished," Cecelia teased, thinking of her several fortune-hunting suitors, "though certainly none capable of cooking their own trout."

Cecelia glanced up, surprised to find the duke's expression had become quite tight. "Come, Your Grace, you are being much too serious. You should take off your boots."

"What?"

Cecelia giggled. "You look tense and it is quite relaxing to be barefoot. Here, sit down." Cecelia pushed him lightly toward a nearby rock.

"Amber—what on earth are you doing?" Julian stared as she knelt before him.

"Taking off your boots, of course."

The duke chuckled, forgetting his ill temper as he watched the red-haired minx tug at his Hessians. "With a bit of training, you would not make a bad valet," he said when she finally managed to remove one.

Cecelia gave him an arch look. "When I finish we must wade across the stream. I saw a lovely clump of blue flowers over there and—" she set the second boot aside and turned back to his stocking feet.

"And?" The duke raised his brows inquiringly when she stopped.

Though she had many times removed her father's boots and stockings, Cecelia suddenly found the idea of stripping this man's legs to the bare skin entirely too personal.

"And um, I should like to see them closer." Standing, she completed her sentence awkwardly.

"You did not finish your job?" Julian reminded her with a curious glance.

"You can finish." Cecelia walked to the edge of the stream. "There are stones quite near the surface here we can cross on."

"No, wait Amber!" The duke stripped his stockings off quickly and started toward her.

"Julian!"

The duke caught Cecelia just as her feet slipped and swung her easily into his arms.

"What on earth happened?" Cecelia flushed at suddenly finding herself cradled against him.

"The moss on those rocks is quite slippery," Julian laughed, carrying her carefully on across the stream. "You must keep to the sand. Are you all right now?" He set her down before him.

"Yes." Cecelia looked away with an embarrassed laugh. "Or at least I shall be if the earth does not fly from beneath me again."

"Well, just in case it does—" the duke took her hand and tucked it over his arm as they continued their walk. The woman was truly an enigma, one moment blithely speaking about other lovers and the next embarrassed at removing a man's socks? And she had become flustered as a maiden when he carried her.

"Look, they are bluebells!"

The duke watched as Cecelia moved from him to pick several of the flowers.

"They have a delightful scent." She turned, holding the flowers up for him to test.

Julian laughed. "You shall make me sneeze. Here." Taking the blossoms from her he tucked them into the disarray of her auburn curls. "Though they should be

roses"—the duke's fingers stilled in the warm silk, as
she looked up at him—"for a lady so lovely." He bent
toward her.

Cecelia sighed unconsciously as the duke's lips lin-
gered but moments on hers before he stepped away.

"Now, come along and I shall show you the waterfall."
Julian smiled to himself at the frustration in her eyes,
confident his Amber should not keep him waiting much
longer.

"Oh Julian, it is beautiful here," Cecelia gasped, looking about the cool, vine-draped bower where the stream
cascaded down to form a wide, clear pool before them.

"This was once one of my favorite places."

"And no slippery rocks!" Cecelia laughed, lifting her
skirts slightly to wade into the crystal water.

"Come along," she invited. "It is quite shallow."

The duke glanced wryly down at his wet trouser legs.
"I might as well. I have already consigned these to the
poor box."

Neither of them noticed the clouds moving in as they
padded about in the shallows, enthusiastically investigating the various small fish and water plants.

"It begins to deepen here, I suppose we must go
back." Cecelia gathered her skirts more carefully, as
she turned from the narrow stream bed she had been
investigating.

"Yes. So it appears," the duke agreed blandly, not
moving from where he blocked the stream. "And the
banks are quite slippery."

"Julian, what are you talking about. Go back, my
skirts are going to get wet." Cecelia looked up at him
impatiently.

"They definitely would, and it'd be a pity to spoil
such a delightful gown," he laughed, raising her chin.
"So I should continue to hold them, were I you."

"*Julian!* You are taking advantage," Cecelia protested, laughing as his head lowered to hers.

"Yes, I know."

The duke had intended but a teasing kiss but as she laughed against his lips he felt a sweet yearning sweep over him that had nothing really to do with passion.

"My darling." Scarcely realizing he had murmured the endearment, the duke drew her against him.

Cecelia forgot her gown, her arms sliding naturally around the duke's neck.

The flash of lightning and spattering of large rain drops some moments later brought the two quickly back to earth.

"Good heavens, where did this come from?" Julian looked up in amazement at the dark sky.

"The 'good heavens,' I would expect." Cecelia giggled, and then glanced down, "Oh no, would you look at my skirts!"

Laughing, the duke swung her easily up into his arms. "I'm not going to say I'm sorry, but I will get you back to the carriage before we are both altogether soaked."

"Well, if you insist." Cecelia snuggled contentedly against him as he strode back toward the others.

"Miss Amber!" Hannah rushed to meet them but the duke waved her aside.

"Amber is fine. One of you boys go back down there and recover my boots," he ordered over his shoulder to the groom and postilion who were hastily gathering the picnic items.

Alvin held the carriage door in the now pelting rain for the duke and Amber to climb inside.

"I'm sorry sweetheart, you are thoroughly drenched."

"So it would seem."

Cecelia colored on glancing down to find the bodice

of her light gown clinging to her with near transparency, but the duke didn't seem to even notice as he brought out a carriage blanket and wrapped it anxiously about her. "Hopefully this shall keep you from getting a chill.

"Here." To the abigail's surprise the duke pulled the second blanket from the carriage rack and handed it to her as she nervously entered the carriage with the two of them. "I fear you've gotten even wetter than your mistress."

"Thank you, Your Grace," Hannah murmured, carefully looking out the window as the duke drew Cecelia against him.

Chapter Eleven

"Wait here, miss, I will fetch an umbrella," Hannah advised, jumping out when the duke's carriage pulled up before Cecelia's house.

"My dear, I want you to go in immediately and take a warm bath to ward off any chill," the duke instructed Cecelia, brushing back a long soaked strand of hair that was laying across the blanket about her. "Just keep wrapped in that blanket until you are—by your fire."

Cecelia glanced up at the duke's broken sentence to find him considering a long red dye mark where he had lifted her hair from the white wool blanket. "Oh dear, I'm sorry."

"You color your hair?" The duke seemed unduly interested in the long strand of hair he held.

"Well, I have used henna to—add highlights," Cecelia managed in embarrassment.

"It appears this henna added more than mere highlights." The duke chuckled, moving the long strand to where she could see it.

"Oh." Cecelia was startled to see the blanket had quite soaked all the color from that particular strand, leaving nothing but a straight lock of her own golden blond hair in his fingers.

"This is your natural color?"

"Well, yes," she reluctantly admitted. "I—that is, Percival and I thought auburn hair more appropriate to the role of Justine."

"Hm." The duke studied her.

Knowing he was trying to picture her with straight blond hair, Cecelia shivered dramatically, wrapping the blanket yet higher about her chin. "Forgive me, but I expect I really should go in."

"Of course, my dear." Julian was instantly contrite. "Here's Hannah with an umbrella now." The duke took her hand and raised it to his lips. "I wish you to rest tonight and shall see you tomorrow."

The duke wandered into his own quarters some time later so lost in thought that he took little note of his valet's horror on seeing the state of his clothing.

"Oh, my heavens, Your Grace!" Morris gasped. "Whatever has happened?"

"What? Oh, we were caught in the storm. Is my bath ready?" Idly stripping the once pristine white shirt from his body, Julian looked down at it and smiled on seeing the same tell-tale smudges of red staining the front.

A blond was she? Somehow her auburn hair, though provocative, never had seemed quite right. But with blond hair, particularly that rich golden strand of silk he had held—

Julian sighed in pleasure at the tantalizing mental vision. He would definitely insist that Amber ceased dyeing her hair once the play concluded. He recalled his first sight of her in the deep rose gown and how it complemented her fair skin even with the red hair. How much more lovely she would have been gowned in rose, but with that pale gold hair.

"Your Grace, I fear that I shall never get this stain from your shirt."

The duke ignored his valet's soulful comments, and climbed into the hip bath to relax in the soothing warm water. The woman was absolutely perfect, except for that bloody Levison. The duke's brow furrowed on thinking of the playwright.

Glancing over at his master's silence, Morris took the frown to be inspired by his comment on the shirt. "But I shall certainly do my best, Your Grace," he advised anxiously. "Perhaps the stain will depart, if treated immediately. May I take it now, sir?"

"Yes, yes," Julian agreed impatiently to whatever the man was babbling about. Not even aware of Morris scurrying out the door, the duke's thoughts returned to Cecelia.

After today, it was plain Amber no longer pined for Levison. The duke's eyes darkened in pleasure on thinking of her sweet weight against him the whole trip back. Surely she would not keep him waiting much longer? Perhaps he should proceed to direct Barnstock to find some country cottage to let for her.

No, Julian smiled to himself in decision. He would buy her a house. That way he could doubtless find something much nicer—had not the Earl of Burton mentioned ridding himself of that bit of property bordering Stanford? It seemed there was some type of residence upon it.

Suddenly impatient to be about the matter, the duke rose from his bath. Burton had a standing card game at White's every weekend, perhaps he could catch him there. The duke frowned at finding his valet had left.

"Morris!"

"Yes, Your Grace?" The valet rushed back in, still holding the shirt he had been anxiously scrubbing.

"I shall be going to White's and—what are you doing with that shirt?" Julian frowned.

"I was rubbing it with ash, Your Grace, and the stain does appear to be lightening."

"For heaven's sakes, man, throw that thing in the rubbish and fetch my clothes."

"But—"

"Now, if you please, Morris. I wish to catch Lord Burton before he leaves for the evening."

"Of course, Your Grace." The valet sighed laying aside the shirt he'd been frantically trying to clean. If only the man would make up his mind.

At about the same time, Cecelia was also enjoying a warming bath. Much as the duke's valet fussed over his clothes, her abigail was fussing over her mistress's behavior, and with even less effect.

"I just could not believe my eyes when I saw you letting that man carry you like that. I thought surely you'd been hurt, and then, there you were, all cuddled up against him all the way home."

"Hannah. Hannah," Cecelia sighed. "Should you not tend to that mote in your own eye first? Or perhaps, I should say, your coachman's eye. I could have sworn I saw you equally all cuddled up in Alvin's arms when I happened to glance your way, did I not?"

Hannah sniffed. "Now miss, you know very well no lady of quality can do what I can. And, what you thought you saw, was likely nothing but an innocent kiss."

"Just one?" Cecelia raised her brows and her abigail giggled, forgetting the scolding.

"Oh miss, I do believe that Alvin is the finest man I have ever met! In fact," she sighed, "I think I just might well be in love!"

"Me too." Cecelia's soft murmur, however, did not hold near the happiness of her abigail's.

"But enough of that." Hannah fortunately did not hear her mistress's comment. "Now we must get your hair re-colored. Do you realize how much of it has quite washed out? I hope His Grace didn't notice."

At White's, the Duke of Stanford received some curious looks as he moved directly toward the card room since he seldom engaged in gambling.

"Burton," Julian was pleased to so easily find the man. "I had hoped to find you here tonight."

"Indeed?" the earl questioned. He was one of the duke's father's close friends, and though amicable with Julian, not someone Stanford usually sought out.

"I had thought to discuss a matter with you this evening, if I might?"

"Of course, I shall be finished here after this hand." Lord Burton smiled, gesturing to a seat in their ongoing round of Brag. "Join us, it is rare you allow us a chance at the coffers of Stanford. Shall we raise the stakes gentlemen?"

"Not on my account, please," the duke smiled, accepting the invitation.

"No, we insist," Viscount Talbot laughed, quickly shuffling the cards. "Club rules, if you please. Ace and nine of diamonds, and jack of clubs are the braggers. Ante—say, a monkey?"

Talbot began dealing as the £500 markers were tossed

casually on the table. "I do say, Stanford, one would not have expected to find you out and about on such a delightfully rainy afternoon."

At the duke's inquiring glance the man chuckled. "Unless the latest *on-dit* errs, that lovely little songbird of *Justine* has moved to your keeping. No offense, Burton, but I should not think I would have need of your company had I that delightful minx awaiting me! Or perhaps," he suggested, turning back to Julian, "the lass is not as talented in all areas as she is on the stage?"

The duke gave the man a cool look, but realized Talbot had given him the perfect chance to see just who these nobles Amber had mentioned were. "You do not know? Why Talbot, with your reputation, I should have thought you acquainted with the talents of every *fille de joie* in London," he commented dryly.

The viscount preened at what he considered a compliment.

"Unfortunately not that one, my dear fellow," he chuckled, "doubtless she must be new to the sisterhood."

"I shouldn't think so," the duke considered his cards, "as she mentioned having previously known a number of nobles."

Lord Burton glanced at the duke in astonishment. Stanford never spoke about his female liaisons, ladies or otherwise.

"The woman told you that?" Talbot looked up, somewhat disconcerted at the information. "I cannot imagine who they might be? Or perhaps she's an émigré, and spoke of French nobility?"

"No, she is quite obviously British," Julian insisted, "though perhaps from the northern shires." He allowed a bored tone into his voice as he made his next wager.

"Impossible!" His mind quite away from his cards, Talbot recklessly tossed out additional notes to match and raise Julian's bet, though Burton and the other players had discreetly all dropped out on the duke's continued raising of the pot. "Were she from the north, Stokesburn would have known about her." He named one of England's more notorious rakes.

"Stokesburn has seen her?" Julian looked up curiously.

"Well, yes. He was in London last week and attended the play particularly for that purpose. He knows every cyprian worth bothering with in the north and insisted she was new."

"Indeed?"

"In fact, he was quite disappointed to find you had already taken the ladybird."

"But you say Stokesburn did not know of her? Perhaps he simply failed to recognize her. You know how women can change their looks." Julian persisted, recalling her blond hair.

"No, I can assure you that Stokesburn would know her if he'd seen her before," Talbot firmly declared. "Quite beyond her exceptional beauty, your Amber has an interesting, almost ladylike quality that quite sets her apart. I know, I should certainly not forget her anytime soon. Uh, are you going to bet?" Talbot realized in sudden dismay the large number of notes he'd recklessly placed on the table.

"Hm." In satisfaction of the man's disclosure, the duke turned his mind to the game. His bets had not been just to keep Talbot talking. In hold cards he had an ace, nine of diamonds and jack of clubs. Combined with his show cards of an additional ace, and two kings, he realized the hand would not likely be surpassed, regardless of what his last card might be.

"Well, what shall it be, Stanford?" Talbot asked nervously after dealing the final card.

Julian scarce missed Talbot's anxiety as he picked up the third card the man dealt him. He hesitated but then in sudden charity with the world in general, Julian folded the hand face down. "This doesn't appear to be my game today." He stood as the relieved viscount happily gathered in his winnings.

"Gentlemen, you'll excuse us? Have you dined, sir?" He turned to Lord Burton.

"What in the devil was that all about in there?" Once the two were ensconced in a private corner of White's dining room, the Earl of Burton turned to Julian. "That is not like you, Stanford, to be discussing your mistress over a card table?"

The duke tried to dissuade the earl with a haughty look. "I beg your pardon, sir?"

"Come now Stanford," the man merely chuckled, pouring them both a glass of port, "those airs will not work with someone who dawdled you on his knee when you were yet in nappies. Now, why on earth did you go out of your way to satisfy that rakehell's curiosity?"

The duke gave in good naturedly. "Very well, if you must know. I was actually satisfying my own curiosity about Amber's comment on knowing other nobles."

"Hm." The earl considered his port idly. "I suppose I can understand it would be annoying to find half of your peers had also bedded your mistress, but by all accounts, you have had her in your keeping some sennight. Is it not a bit late for such concerns?"

"Nonetheless, I am glad they had not." Julian avoided the question. "Now, what I wished to speak to you about, was that bit of property that marches with Stanford, you once mentioned. Do you yet wish to sell it?"

The earl nodded, dropping the other matter. "That

parcel was the dower house of the countess's mother. Since she passed on, I have no use for it. It is but a bother to keep in repair."

"It has been years since I have ridden that way, but I seem to recall it had a pleasant residence?" Julian inquired politely as they placed their orders with the waiter.

"Yes. Not grand by your standards, but rather nicely appointed," the earl obliged. "Six bedrooms, banquet and family dining, two or perhaps three parlours, if I recall—and the usual complement of stables and the like. And it's by the sea." The earl named his price.

Julian considered for a moment. This was definitely more than he would normally think of purchasing for a mistress, but for Amber . . .

A slow smile touched the duke's lips, as he thought in pleasure of her surprise. He would furnish it for her of course, and set up the stable so they might take rides along the sea.

"Would you care to ride out to see it?"

"Oh yes. Of course," Julian brought his thoughts back to the present. "Perhaps we might go tomorrow?"

"I do apologize, as I must be out of town and should not be able to accompany you tomorrow, but you are welcome to go on your own, if you do not mind?"

"That will be fine," Julian agreed, having actually intended the "we" to be him and Amber.

"Excellent." Lord Burton smiled. "I will advise the caretaker of your arrival. I would expect you have the place in mind for some relative?"

"No, I had thought to put Amber out there," Julian answered absently.

"Your mistress!" The earl's brow furrowed in disbelief. "Surely you jest, sir?"

The duke's look cooled. "If you find that objectionable, I am sure I can find another property."

"By Jove, Stanford," the older man snapped. "That is not the point. I could not care a whit whether you bought the place to burn it! But to establish one's mistress on a property, right next to your own?"

"I expect my relationship with Amber will be of sufficient duration to merit it," Julian supplied, his tone clearly intended to end the matter but the earl would not be forestalled.

"My good fellow," Lord Burton said anxiously. "I am aware that I tread on our families' long-standing friendship by even saying this, but are you certain you are not losing sight of reality?"

"Reality? I fear I do not see your point?" With effort, the duke contained his growing ire.

"About this Amber. The ton is abuzz with how you are at every single performance of that play, take her out every evening, even to your own home to dine. And just now, this concern on her past lovers! Julian," the man hesitated. "I well recall how easy it is to become infatuated with someone like your Amber, but do not forget, regardless how enchanting, the woman is a prostitute."

The earl sighed as Julian merely gave him a cold look.

"Stanford, it is painfully obvious that you do not wish to discuss this matter, but I am only saying what your own father would, were he yet alive. This establishing of Amber in such a manner is beyond foolish. Is it not even cruel to her, to give her expectations of this long term relationship? I cannot imagine you would continue with a mistress once you decide to wed."

The duke's tone by now, was barely civil. "I cannot see how it concerns you, sir, but I have no plans for taking a bride in the near future."

"I am aware it is none of my concern." The earl refused to take affront. "But it is your mother's. I may add that despite the duchess's constant plea that I speak with you on the matter, I had not intention of doing so, at least until now."

"Lord Burton—"

The earl, however, waved the younger man to silence. "Kindly recall, Julian, you are the only heir to the dukedom and what, two-and-thirty now? I am certain you do not require either your mother or myself to tell you that you should be seeking a duchess and establishing your nursery, not settling in for an extended relationship with a new mistress. Or have you no wish to see your own children grown?"

The duke laid his napkin down and stood. "If you would be so good as to excuse me."

The other members of the card game were just entering the dining room as Julian nodded curtly to the earl and left.

"Stanford's mood certainly changed." Talbot glanced after the departing duke.

"Yes, may we hope for the wiser," the earl muttered, ignoring the other lord's curious glance at his comment. "As Julian has abandoned me, might I join you gentlemen at a larger table?"

The duke tooled his phaeton back to the Stanford town house some time later in an inexplicably bleak mood. As much as he hated admitting it, Burton was right.

Julian wasn't at all sure when, but at some point his feeling toward Amber had changed perceptibly. Though he had previously been rather fond of other mistresses for a time, he had neither felt this sweet, warm feeling of protectiveness that Amber inspired, nor the almost unreasoning jealousy on the very thought of her belonging to anyone else, when she obviously already had belonged, at least to her bloody playwright. He had to get the woman out of his mind and put the whole matter back into perspective.

"Have you sent the answers to those invitations I gave you yesterday?" the duke curtly inquired of his steward the following morning.

"I fear I have not yet finished with all of them, Your Grace, but I shall see to—"

"Bring them back to me."

"Of course." Barnstock quickly returned with the usual week's stack of invitations to various come-outs, balls and soirees which the duke almost always declined except on the rare occasion that it was a particular friend's daughter being presented. Since the duke hadn't dismissed him, he stood waiting while Stanford flipped almost angrily through the stack before selecting out several for each of the following days.

"Send acceptances for these." He brusquely handed the letters back.

"Acceptances, Your Grace?" The man raised his brows in surprise.

"Yes. And, take a letter—"

The following morning Cecelia's happy anticipation for the day was crushed on receiving a very formal missive from the duke's steward that His Grace would not be stopping by for luncheon after all.

"The duke doubtless just had some other engagement," Hannah assured Cecelia hoping to lighten her spirits, though she herself was relieved her mistress was not to be subjected to what she feared was a dangerously developing situation.

All the household staff however became concerned when a hired hackney, rather than one of the duke's own coaches arrived to take Amber to the theater.

"Amber, are you sure you are all right?" Vivian asked in concern. The other players had tactfully refrained from remarking on Amber's arrival in the hired vehicle or the duke's pointed absence during the morning performance, though they all knew he was back in town.

"Of course, I am fine," Cecelia managed convincingly, though her spirits drooped even more when the duke's box again remained empty for the matinee performance.

Though hiding her hurt, Cecelia could not hide her alarm over what the loss of Julian's presence meant. At the end of play she was besieged by a horde of aspiring new suitors who had already heard that the duke had changed his mind on her.

Cecelia was almost in tears when Daniel managed to spirit her out the back of the theater.

"What are you complaining about, Amber? That just shows how popular you are," Vivian said, as the cast members who had crowded into the carriage moved over obligingly to let her in.

Cecelia did not even try to hide her distress. "Oh Viv, I do not know if I can handle this even another three nights!"

"You'll get over your duke. I know it hurts, it always does. But someone else will come along—" At Amber's anguished look, the other actress sighed. "Well, anyway," she changed her direction. "You do not have to worry. We will keep these rakes away from you after the next performances."

"Right, love," Daniel and the others readily agreed.

"And, I'm sure you'll be all right once the play's over and you can get away from all this for a spell."

When she arrived home Cecelia's megrims were somewhat alleviated on finding a thick missive from Percival awaiting her.

> Dear Sissy:
>
> Forgive me for not contacting you sooner but you may now share in our jubilation. We have a baby daughter. Elizabeth Constance was born two days ago. She is a beautiful little lady, and I thank God that both she and Constance enjoy blessed good health. I cannot wait to introduce my little Liz to my wonderful cousin, who has made it possible now for me to support my family in a respectable manner.
>
> In case you don't know, Stanford's solicitor has been in contact, and I cannot believe the amount of moneys he has in trust for me, even after subtracting all funds owed to Stanford. I cannot thank you enough, my love, for the success of *Justine* which would not have been possible without you.
>
> You will be pleased to know, Stanford has given his leave for a full production of my plays next year at the Barcelly and subscriptions are already almost sold out. Though doubtless the patrons will be disappointed to find the new star of the stage has gone into retirement, I can only hope my humble plays can survive without you.

Cecelia smiled as she scanned through the rest of the long letter telling of Percival and Constance's excitement on being new parents. They had already found a nearby farm to purchase with a "wonderfully large manor that Constance plans to quite fill with children."

"And, my dear," Cecelia was pleasantly surprised to read, "you need not worry about Wally and Martha. I've told Constance all about them and she has decreed that I must bring them back with me since we shall be needing servants in the house."

"Oh Hannah," Cecelia sighed on finishing the letter. "I shall be so glad to get out of the whole situation and back to my own life."

"Of course, my lady," her abigail agreed, though she knew her mistress was not telling the whole truth. "Since the play ends Friday, should I begin packing?"

"Yes, I suppose that is a good idea. Percival said he will be here for the last night's performance, and then would escort us back to Somersett. I would like to be ready to leave immediately after the play."

"What shall we do with the duke's possessions?" Hannah asked carefully.

"Have them packed and returned to His Grace." Cecelia turned away to stare bleakly out the narrow window. "I have a dreadful headache, Hannah. Would you mind fetching me something for it?" she asked mainly for a few minutes alone.

Three more days. If only she could get through them and return to the peace and sanity of Somersett.

How had she let herself fall in love with a duke, who only wanted her for his mistress! "And one whose interest she could not even keep in that regard!" Cecelia added wryly to herself. Though Amber likely fared better with Julian than Baroness Somersett would have. Even had she met him as a lady the duke would not have been interested in a baroness of some debt ridden estate—and certainly not one already into her twenties, Cecelia told herself morosely, recalling what she had overheard just that afternoon.

The Countess Blackmon had bragged quite loudly

during intermission how the Duke of Stanford had
changed his mind after declining and accepted an invitation to her darling little Priscella's very first ball,
doubtless after seeing the child at Lord Hamvil's soiree.

The duke was as deeply in megrims as Cecelia.

Appalled at the simpering young misses practically
thrust upon him by the machinations of their mothers,
Julian had not stayed past the requisite time at any
function attended the last two days.

However, that evening was the Earl of Blackmon's
daughter's ball and the girl had indeed caught the
duke's eye. An absolutely stunning confection of ivory
skin and ebony hair, the girl was truly a diamond of the
first water. Julian had decided she was at least worth
meeting.

However, after five minutes of the celebrated Miss
Herville's charming blushes, tinkling laughter, and gay
pratterings, the duke began to wonder what the chit
was doing out of the schoolroom. Though she was presumably of an age to marry, the very idea of taking such
a mere girl to wife was an abhorrence and he again
departed early.

"Did you have a pleasant night, Your Grace?" Barnstock greeted his employer at his return that evening.

The duke did not bother with an answer. "Kindly
send my regrets on the remainder of those bloody invitations I had you accept! Surely, I must have been out of
my mind!"

"Yes, sir." At Julian's raised brow, his steward quickly
amended, "That is, of course, I will send your regrets,
sir."

The duke smiled wryly. "You were probably right the first time." He tugged his cravat loose in irritation. "I guess I have never before given the matter much thought, Barnstock, but these last days have shown me just how disgusting the whole marriage mart atmosphere of our so-called *haut ton* is."

Julian poured himself a liberal portion of whiskey to try to drown the distaste of the evening. "The mothers at these functions, all but selling their own daughters to the most prestigious bidder. And those girls, scarce more than children, trading their virginity to some man thrice their age oft for naught but a title."

The duke's steward remained tactfully silent as Julian sighed. "It might behoove one to wonder if there is much difference between such marriages and the arrangement of a man and his mistress, except perhaps that the latter is more honest."

His mind moving as usual back to Cecelia, the duke glanced automatically at the mantel clock.

"The hell with it," he muttered determinedly setting his glass down. "Tell Ayers to have my coach brought back around."

Chapter Twelve

"Thank you, but Wally will have dinner ready at home," Cecelia said, declining the other cast members' usual invitation to join them for a late supper after the production.

Daniel glanced worriedly about the quickly emptying theatre lot. "If you are sure, but I don't want to leave you here alone, Amber. Has your hackney arrived?"

"Yes, it is over by the trees there." Cecelia gestured. "Thank you, but I will be fine. I am leaving now as well."

"All right. Good night then, love." Daniel waved and ran to join the others already loading into another hackney.

"I am pleased to see you did not join your fellow players."

"Lord Bexton!" Cecelia gasped as the man stepped from the shadows. "My heavens sir, you startled me."

"I am sorry, my dear. That was not my intention," the earl chuckled, taking her hand. "But since you are alone, perhaps I might request the pleasure of your company at dinner.''

"That is kind of you, sir," Cecelia said carefully, "but I must decline." She tried to remove her hand from his but he held it more firmly. "If you will forgive me, my lord, I have a carriage waiting."

"It does not appear so," Bexton laughed, nodding to where the hired vehicle was just departing.

"Oh no! Wait, driver!" Cecelia waved at the coachman in alarm, but he continued from the lot without pause. "Oh my heavens, why did he do that?"

"I must confess, I took the liberty of having my man pay the driver off," Bexton advised in amusement. "Now you needn't worry, my dear, you shall be much more comfortable in my carriage than that hired equipage."

"Lord Bexton, you had no right to dismiss my carriage!" Cecelia tried to keep the fear from her voice as the last coaches pulled from the dark courtyard. "I am really quite tired and wish to go home. Now I must insist that you excuse me." She managed to free her hand from his grip and turned away. If she could just get back inside the theater—

The earl caught her shoulder, stopping her. "No, I do not believe I shall excuse you"—he pulled her roughly against him—"though I will gladly take you to where you can—rest."

Nauseated at the foul smell of spirits on his breath, Cecelia struggled to free herself from his superior strength in growing panic. The man was inebriated!

"My lord, please, let go of me!"

"No."

She gasped as the earl pinned her arms behind her, barely managing to evade his seeking lips.

The earl laughed unpleasantly. "I begin to see why

Stanford tired of you so soon, Amber, but you will find I have more patience. Gordon, bring the carriage over,'' he called to his coachman.

"No, you cannot do this," Cecelia half sobbed on hearing a carriage, which she assumed was the earl's drawing up.

Cecelia almost fell as Bexton was suddenly spun away from her.

"I do not believe Amber wishes your attentions," Julian snapped coldly, stepping between Cecelia and the earl.

"Stanford? What in the—" the Earl of Bexton sputtered, considerably sobered by the duke's rough handling.

"I think it advisable that you leave, Bexton."

"What the hell is this, Stanford? You had dropped the doxy." Bexton stepped back in alarm as the duke again started toward him.

"All right, all right. You are welcome to the little witch." The earl shrugged nonchalantly in some effort to regain his dignity as he headed to his own carriage. "I can probably do better for my blunt in Covent Garden anyway," he added, once safely out of reach.

The duke muttered an expletive before turning to find Cecelia standing behind him, hugging her arms about herself in shock.

"Amber? Are you all right?"

"Yes—I think," she managed shakily.

Julian took her hands, his eyes glittering angrily at the red marks on her wrists. "Did Bexton hurt you?"

"I'm all right. But thank you for—"

The duke felt her hands tremble in his and with a soft curse drew her into his arms. "Hush, my sweet. I swear that low bastard will never touch you again!" He held her a moment soothingly. "Come now, let me take you home."

Once inside the duke's coach Cecelia tried to regain her composure. "I am terribly sorry, Your Grace, that you had to become involved in—" she began in embarrassment, but Julian cut her off.

"No, Amber, it is I who owe you an apology. This would surely not have happened had I not left you unprotected like that."

"You are not responsible for me, Your Grace," Cecelia looked away in embarrassment, "but I thank you for your help."

Julian reached over and raised her chin, making her look at him.

"I am responsible for you, my dear, because I wish to be. I know I owe you an explanation for leaving."

"Your Grace—"

"No," he quieted her protest. "It was unpardonable of me to just abandon you as I did, without an explanation but—"

Cecelia listened in increasing chagrin as the duke confided his discussion with Lord Burton.

"The man quite infuriated me because he was correct," Julian concluded wryly. "Since we last parted I have attended functions for the season's debutantes with the firm intent of seeking a duchess, but I found I could not even think of any of those children in such a way." Julian knew his words hurt the woman carefully sheltering her gaze from him, but he was determined to be honest with her. "I shall, of course, have to marry eventually, Amber, and whatever my wishes, I would not be unfaithful to my wife." He paused briefly. "But Burton was also correct about you. I do care for you, my dear, more than I have any woman previously. I cannot offer you a lifetime, Amber, but I shall try to see that you are happy the time we have and promise that you shall never lack for anything." He raised her chin, his eyes darkening at the tears he found glistening in hers.

"Julian, please, I—" Cecelia tried, but her voice broke in emotion.

"Hush, my love."

As the duke lowered his head, Cecelia could not deny herself the wonder of his kiss—this last time. Tomorrow Percival would return, *Justine* would end and Amber would exist no longer.

Julian finally realized his coach had been stopped before Amber's house for some minutes.

"Come, my darling, let us go in." Tonight, he had no intention of leaving her.

The duke's groom who had been standing for several minutes quite properly with his back to the carriage, quickly hid his grin and staidly turned to open the door as the duke tapped on it.

Julian stepped out and nodding dismissal to the footman, gave Cecelia his own hand to help her down.

The duke had just started to instruct his coachman to stable the horses when the front door to Amber's house opened.

"Amber?"

"Percival?" Cecelia spun in surprise on hearing her cousin's voice. "It *is* you!" She ran excitedly to meet him as he came toward her. "But I had not expected you until tomorrow evening."

Her cousin drew her into a hug. "I know, but everything at home is going so well, I could not bear leaving you alone any longer. Oh, you don't mind my staying over here tonight, do you love? The lease on my rooms ran out and—" he finally noticed the duke standing coolly to the side. "Oh Stanford. Forgive me, Your

Grace. I was just so happy to see Amber again that I"—
he laughed in embarrassment—"but, do come in. Join
us for supper."

Cecelia felt the duke's eyes on her but could not
bring herself to meet his gaze. "Yes, please."

"Thank you but I must decline," the duke said
blandly.

Cecelia watched in distress as the duke turned coldly
back to his carriage, but Percival in his excitement on
telling her of all that had happened did not notice.

"Come, love." He took her hand and led her up to
the house. "I must tell you about Lizzie."

Julian's bleak mood turned quickly to a boiling rage
as his carriage carried him back to his own manor. So,
his sweet Amber had known Percival was returning on
the morrow? Her greeting of the young playwright left
little to doubt on her continued feelings for the man
not to mention the fact that she had not demurred in
the least on Levison staying the night with her.

What a fool he had been, thinking she cared for him!
Doubtless, the little trollop had just determined to enjoy
his favors, while her lover was away!

The duke rapped angrily on the coach top.

"Your Grace?" the coachman pulled up and leaned
over.

"Take me to my club," the duke ordered unable to
face his thoughts at home alone.

Stanford ignored the gaming room of White's and
took his glass of claret beside the fire. Since several
fellow members of the House of Lords were gathered
there discussing politics, Julian determined it a safe

subject far enough from that which was causing him unaccountable mental anguish. Unfortunately, no sooner had the duke joined into one of the continuing debates on Prinny's exorbitant expenses than a noisy group of inebriated young lords entered.

"Bexton again, and with his cronies this time," Viscount Fairmeadow muttered in aggravation. "He was here earlier but left. I had hoped we were rid of him for the evening."

Stanford glanced up just as the earl spied him.

"Well, if it isn't His Grace," Bexton laughed, heading unsteadily toward them.

"Stanford, should I call—" Fairmeadow began.

"No. I can handle him." Julian hid his irritation as the young man came up.

"Now I don't call this fair play at all, my good fellow." Bexton leaned on a chair to steady himself. "You show up, chase me off that delectable little morsel and then come *here*? What, did your mistress spurn your advances as well? Perhaps, she has already found someone even plumper in the purse?" he chortled in delight.

"You are quite foxed, Bexton, which is probably why Amber did not care for your attentions. I merely took her home. And, she is not my mistress," he added coldly. "As far as I know the woman is back with her playwright."

"Foxed? Yes, I suppose I am," Bexton grinned tipsily. "So she's not your mistress anymore? So does that mean I have Your Grace's permission to take the doxy?" He made a comic bow.

"Come along, Philip," the earl's more sober friend Adderly, urged him away. "Excuse us, Stanford."

The duke considered the departing earl in sudden worry about his remark. Then again, Amber was not his concern, he told himself, she was Levison's. Let him take care of her.

He reached for his claret glass. "How much is this pavilion the prince commissioned Nash to rebuild going to cost England?"

The last night of the play had gone excellently though Cecelia's heart had not been in the production. The play had closed amidst accolades to both cast and playwright.

Cecelia descended the rental house's stairs for the last time, as the final bandboxes were carried down.

"Miss Amber," Hannah still called her by the stage name as there were various post boys about helping with the loading. "Are you quite certain you won't be needing me to go with you?"

Cecelia had decided to go home with Percival to see Constance and their new infant before returning to her own estate.

"I shall be fine with Percival, Hannah. And Martha shall be with us in case I do need anything so I'd really prefer you travel on to Somersett with the baggage and see that the house is in order. You know how Mrs. Grant can be when we are gone."

Hannah grimaced at the mention of Cecelia's elderly housekeeper. "Yes miss, that is probably a good idea. I expect we are about ready to leave then. Wasn't Mr. Levison sending his carriage back?"

"He had an hour or so of final business to attend at Barcelly, before we could leave. I do hope he remembers to send the coach back, as I wish to return these other items to Somersett House before leaving."

"Miss Amber, do you want me to go with you to deliver these things?" Martha asked after Hannah departed.

"No, thank you Martha. I can manage, if you and

Wally will just remain here to finish closing this house. Oh, here comes a carriage now. That must be Percival's."

The carriage however that arrived was a hired hackney. "Coach for Miss Amber." The young driver tugged off his hat as Wally opened the door.

"Miss, did you send for a hackney?" Wally turned to her questioningly.

"No."

"A gentleman had the hackney sent, miss. He said you would know what for," the boy told them.

"Oh, Percy must have just sent a hackney instead of his own coach," Cecelia assumed reaching for her reticule. "These boxes here are to go with me." She directed the driver to load the several cases.

When Wally received a sealed note for Percival some half hour later he thought nothing of it, but merely placed it on the hall table for the playwright when he returned.

It was only a little beyond the lunch hour when Percy bounded into the town house. "Amber? Wally?" He glanced at the table and picked up the letter.

"Yes, sir?" Wally hurried from the kitchen where he and Martha had been having a bit of lunch as no one else was around.

"Where is Ce—Amber? She's probably furious with me, is she not? I forgot about sending the coach for her to use."

"Miss Amber?" Wally looked at him in surprise. "Why she went on to deliver those boxes in the hackney."

"Oh, she got a hackney?" Percy asked absently, slitting open the envelope.

"The hackney you sent, sir," Wally elaborated.

"I sent?" Percival finally began paying attention. "I have not sent any hackney. Surely, she just stopped one or something?" he asked in growing concern.

"No," the butler said firmly. "The boy that came to the door said quite clearly that you had sent it, sir. Or a gentleman, he said. Perhaps you told someone to send it and then forgot?" he tried delicately, well knowing how the playwright was absentminded on occasion.

Percival glared at him. "I did not send a hackney. When did she leave?" he asked anxiously.

"Nigh on about three hours ago, sir."

"Three hours? She should have been back by now! And you've heard nothing?"

"No, sir." The butler recalled the letter Percival still held unread. "I don't suppose that was a message from her? It did come after she left."

Percival quickly unfolded the single sheet. "What in the—?"

"What is it sir?"

"My God!" he cried in alarm. "Who the devil is the Earl of Bexton?" Percival had forgotten the young lord who had visited the theater.

"Bexton? Some young lord, a friend of the duke's I believe. He showed a decided preference for Miss Amber. Even sent her some diamonds and I fear a rather improper note. But His Grace returned them, and I thought most likely discouraged the young man," the butler explained. "What did the man say?"

"He claims Miss Amber has decided to go with him to his country home rather than continuing with me," Percival said grimly.

"Miss Amber went with him?" the butler asked startled.

"Of course she did not," Percival snapped, "at least not willingly. This man is a friend of Stanford? I must find him!'' Percival headed back to his carriage at a run.

Julian had buried himself in some long overdue papers to keep his thoughts from their aggravating tendency of returning to Amber.

"I do not wish to be disturbed until dinner, Ayers," the duke informed his butler. "If anyone comes by, I am not at home."

"Yes, Your Grace." The butler very carefully closed the library door, knowing better than to question his master when he was in one of his rare black moods.

When the playwright arrived frantically at the duke's house some minutes later Ayers informed him his master was out.

"Out? Where? I simply must see him!" Percival assumed the man was telling the truth.

"I am sure I don't know, sir," the butler allowed firmly. "Perhaps if you wish to leave a message?"

"Maybe he's at his club," Percy ran his hand anxiously through his hair. "I'll try there. If His Grace returns, please tell him it is extremely urgent that I speak to him right away."

"Sir," Ayers started to call the man back, wondering if perhaps this was something he should notify the duke of, but Percival had already dashed back to his carriage. Ayers walked to the library door and hesitated several minutes but couldn't quite bring himself to face the duke's ire on being disturbed after specific orders to the contrary. He turned away. Dinner would be in a couple of hours, surely the matter could wait until then.

"The Duke of Stanford?" The doorman of White's surveyed the disheveled young man critically. "The duke is not here at the moment."

"What about Lord Bexton? Earl, I believe. Yes, the Earl of Bexton?" Percival tried again.

"The earl is not at the club either, sir." The doorman started to move away but Percival stopped him.

"Where does this earl live?"

"Sir, we do not give out directions to our member's homes," the man sniffed.

"Please, it is imperative—" Percival found himself facing a closed door and muttering a very uncharacteristic expletive ran back to his carriage. He had tried the Somersett House, but it was apparent that no one had been by there to drop anything off. No one at the theater had heard anything from Cecelia. He'd even been by the duke's solicitor's office but the man was out.

It was some two hours since Percival had first gone to Stanford's house when he again banged on the door.

"Has Stanford returned?" Percival asked anxiously without preamble as Ayers opened the door.

The butler hesitated a moment. "His Grace is occupied." He decided to risk taking a message as the young man seemed so upset. "Perhaps if I—"

"The duke's here? Thank God!" Percival pushed past the butler and into the hallway. "I've been hunting all over London for him. Did you give him my message? Where is he? I must see him right now!"

"Sir! I said I could—"

"Whatever is all this commotion?" Julian demanded, exiting his library. "Levison? What are you doing here?"

"It's Cec—uh, Amber. Your bloody friend Bexton has apparently—"

The duke interrupted tersely. "Perhaps you would come into my library?" He closed the door firmly behind the playwright and gestured him to a seat. "Now, what is this about?"

Percival ignored the chair, glaring as Julian casually went over to the bar. "May I offer you something, sir?"

"No! I'm trying to tell you Amber has been kidnapped!" Percival snapped, quite put out by the man's attitude.

The duke raised an aristocratic brow, at Levison's tone. "Kidnapped? Really, Levison, aren't you being a bit melodramatic? What are you saying? I believe you mentioned Lord Bexton?"

"Your friend, the Earl of Bexton, had a note delivered to me at Amber's house saying that she—oh, here." He pulled the wadded paper from his pocket and handed it to the duke.

Julian read through the brief note and handed it back in disdain. "I should think the matter is patently plain. I am sorry if it is painful to you, but quite obviously the woman has decided to change protectors. There is nothing in that note to decry any type kidnapping."

"No, Your Grace, you do not understand. Amber would never go with that man!" Percival tried desperately. "We were to leave for my home this afternoon. We should have been gone by now; in fact, she was merely going to deliver some things and was supposed to return within the hour. But instead I intercepted this note! She went in a hired hackney that she thought I sent. But I did not!"

Julian sighed. "Listen my friend. I had not wished to tell you this, but as you are so adamant on what the woman would not do, I suppose I must."

"What are you talking about?"

"Your Amber. I am quite sure the woman is willingly in Bexton's company. Doubtless, he merely raised his offer."

"What!"

"He made her an offer to be his mistress previously, but as she knew I was also interested, she declined him."

"He—you" Percival sputtered. "You made Amber a proposition even after our talk!" he shouted.

"Calm yourself, Levison." The duke's cold tone brought the young man back to earth. "Yes, I did, as you had quite apparently abandoned her. And, must I remind you, I was already paying for her expenses!" he added dryly.

Percival groaned, "I know I should not have put the house on your accounts, Stanford, but you knew I would pay you back. And I have, every shilling!"

"Yes, now you have. However, at the time apparently even Amber was unaware that it was I, who was supporting her."

"Oh no, you told her?"

"Yes." The duke took a sip from his scotch to wash the bitter taste from his mouth the conversation seemed to be giving him. "But Amber understood, and agreed to the changed arrangements."

"Agreed to—What are you saying?" Percival stared.

"Quite plainly, Levison, that Amber agreed to become my mistress."

"You are a bloody liar! She would never—"

"If it is of any consolation," the duke continued, merely giving the irate man a warning glance. "She did apparently care for you, as she asked that I be patient in claiming my rights as she felt herself to be in love with you, even though you had abandoned her."

"Oh Sissy!" Percival groaned at what he must have put his cousin through. He then recalled the duke's words in alarm. "She wanted you to be patient—so you did not—that is—you—"

"No, I did not," the duke allowed curtly. "Your

Amber is also rather adept at getting people to do her bidding."

"I know that only too well," Percival agreed grimly. "But we have got to find her, *immediately*. Where does Bexton live?"

"Levison, I thought I had made it plain the woman is with Bexton of her own free will. Give her up, and return to your wife," he curtly advised.

"Damn it Stanford," Percival ignored the duke's thunderous expression. "She is *not* with the man willingly. Trust me. You have to help me save her!"

The duke turned and walked to the bell pull. "I have no intentions of involving myself further with your mistress." He pulled on the summons. "Now I fear I'm finding this conversation quite tedious. I am sure Ayers will show you out."

The butler appeared instantly to hold the door open.

"Stanford, you can't do this! This Bexton is your friend, I have to know how to find him," Percival begged desperately.

"Ayers, the gentleman is leaving." The duke moved pointedly back to his desk.

"Oh God." Percival groaned as the duke's very stalwart butler came purposefully toward him. "Stanford, Amber is *not* my mistress. She is my cousin, Lady Cecelia Somersett."

"What? What did you say?" Julian spun around.

The butler didn't need to be told to leave, and closed the door.

"This—none of this was supposed to happen," Percival managed, raking his hand through his already disheveled hair. "Sissy was just—just helping me out with *Justine* because that bloody Miriam left me in the lurch and—she, well, posed as my mistress to dissuade the possible approach of—"

"Lady Cecelia?" the duke interrupted in disbelief.

"Yes. Baroness, actually," Percival rushed on, "but Sissy has never been married. It is her title by right. So you see, Stanford, Cecelia is truly quite innocent. There is certainly no circumstance under which she would ever willingly go off with any man like that."

"Oh, my God!" The duke finally began to understand a lot of things. "What in the devil ever possessed you to ask a lady, your own cousin, to get involved in something like this?" He turned on the startled playwright in fury.

"I would never have asked her to do such!" Percival defended himself. "Actually, I went to Sissy, thinking she might know of some actress, one who could sing and the next thing I know—somehow—she had talked me into this!" he admitted morosely. "I know that seems impossible but—"

"No," Julian quipped wryly. "I rather expect I know just what you mean. Ayers!" he bellowed. "Come Levison, we must find Am—Lady Cecelia, immediately!"

Chapter Thirteen

Cecelia's soulful thoughts so preoccupied her mind once she entered the hackney that it was quite some time before she realized they had been riding for longer than it should have taken to reach Somersett House.

"Coachman?" She tapped on the roof of the carriage to no avail. Was the man deaf? He had doubtless taken a wrong turn somewhere and he was driving much too fast!

Cecelia pulled back the carriage curtain and gasped. There was nothing but fields and hedgerows outside the carriage! Where was the man going?

"Coachman!" she yelled louder, quite sure now that he must hear her, but the man merely whipped his horses even faster.

What was happening? Had the fool gone insane? Surely he could not be planning to kidnap her? As far as anyone knew, she was merely an actress, not someone to hold for ransom or any such. Cecelia cried aloud as the coach barreled around a corner flinging her hard against the door. Good heavens, the man was going to wreck them!

"Coachman, stop the carriage this instant!" she ordered but the man merely cracked his whip over the horses yet again.

"Oh my!" The carriage careened over a small bridge, causing Cecelia to bounce clear up to the ceiling. The idiot was going to kill them all! Perhaps it would be wiser not to risk angering him she decided, holding on tightly.

At least when she remained quiet the coachman allowed his horses to settle back to a steady pace. She looked out to try to discern where they were, but nothing seemed familiar.

She could perhaps jump out, but the coach was still going so fast that at best she would probably break her neck. No, she would just have to wait and see where they were taking her. Maybe it was really just a mistake.

A few minutes later, the coachman turned the hackney into the courtyard of an old inn, and two other men came out.

"All right, out of there, missy," a coarse voice ordered as the door swung open.

"Who are you?" Cecelia stared at the rough peasants. "I demand to be returned to London!"

One man merely laughed. "I am the innkeeper, here." A dirty hand grabbed her wrist and pulled her out of the carriage. "And you shall be returned to London, least soon as the cove's satisfied of you."

At Cecelia's look of horror, surprisingly the man's voice softened, "Now you ain't needn' to be so scared, missy," he advised. "Bexton ain't really a bad 'un. 'e ain't go 'urt ya none."

"Bexton? The *Earl* of Bexton had you do this!" Cecelia gasped.

"You didn't know you'd done caught ye'rself an earl's eye?" the man grinned, misunderstanding. "Well, you just treat 'em nice tonight sweet, and you'll be on yer way tomorrow with a much plumper purse." He winked knowingly. " 'E's brought some of the sisterhood out 'ere before, so I can vouch on it, I can."

Cecelia thought frantically. "Is—Bex—his lordship," she changed carefully, "here yet?"

"So now you're impatient?" The man laughed. "He ain't here yet, but 'e'll be along. You come on with me. I got you a nice room, clean sheets o' fine linen and all."

"You better watch that 'un. 'Is lordship'll be mighty mad you let anything 'appen to 'er," the coachman warned the other man as he climbed down from the carriage.

It was quite apparent to Cecelia that between the three strong men, her best chance lay in lowering their guard by appearing willing.

She sniffed pretentiously, shaking her skirts out as though nothing were wrong. "You are a fine one to give warnings." She glared at the coachman. "After practically killing us both on the road! I must be bruised all over. Why didn't you just tell me the earl had sent for me?"

The man's eyes narrowed suspiciously. "Well fancy that, will you! Bexton said you wouldn't be all that agreeable. Fact is, 'e said it was 'aving some little bit of an actress turnin' 'im down, that riled 'im enough so's 'e 'ad us fetch you out 'ere. Now, just why is that, do you suppose?"

Cecelia shrugged. "The man grabbed at me outside the theater where I work. He was altogether foxed. How was I to know he was an *earl*. And besides, I already had an appointment," she smiled flirtatiously, putting a bit of cockney into her own speech. "Now, is there somewhere I might freshen up a bit, before his lordship arrives? You know how particular the gentry is?" If she could just make them trust her.

The innkeeper gave a gap-toothed grin and gestured her to follow him. "Come along then. I'll show ya' the way, as 'es liable to be here soon and we wouldn't want to be disappointin' him."

"Thank you," Cecelia said sweetly. Glancing covertly back to where the driver and third man stood by the coach, she suddenly had an idea.

"Oh, those boxes," she indicated the cases destined for Somersett House, "they were to go to my last protector's cousin's house, but as he's dismissed me, it wouldn't bother me a bit if someone else wanted the things in them."

"That's right kind of you."

The innkeeper looked over sharply as the other two men began eagerly climbing up after the boxes. "Now that ain't quite fair. I got me a lass'd like some pretties too. You run on along upstairs, missy. You can't miss the room, it's to the right," he gestured vaguely before trotting back to the coach. "You fellows wait now."

Cecelia glanced around the interior of the small inn, just long enough to be sure there was no one else there before heading out the rear door. She considered a small copse of woods directly behind the inn, but wasn't that where they would expect her to run?

The duke's jaw tightened ominously. "What do you mean, you don't know where Lord Bexton is?" He glowered at the man's butler and steward standing nervously before him. "I cannot imagine the man leaving town for the night without a mention of his direction."

"His lordship had a private appointment," the butler finally allowed carefully. "I am certain, Your Grace, that he will be back in the morning, if you have need of him."

"This matter will not wait until morning," the duke snapped. "I assure you, your employer will not thank you for keeping me from finding him immediately." Which, was quite true. If he found Bexton before Cecelia was harmed he just might not kill the bastard!

The earl's two men looked at one another questioningly. "Very well," the steward finally decided. "If it is that important. I believe Lord Bexton has some property he owns about an hour out on the old North road. It hosts a small inn where he entertains on occasion."

Stanford's countenance tightened. Just an hour away. And Cecelia had been gone for three hours.

"I believe I know where that is," he managed to hide his dismay. "I assume Bexton has been gone long enough that I will not interrupt his entertaining?"

"Actually, his lordship just left some half hour past," the butler replied. "He was to have left much earlier, but was delayed by a business matter."

The butler raised a brow to the steward as the duke spun without a word and slammed out the door.

"Did they tell you?" Percival anxiously inquired as the duke leaped back on his phaeton.

"Yes." Julian told Percival what he had learned while tooling his team expertly about on the narrow street. "And, fortunately he is only a half hour ahead of us.

"Now, my little *Amber,* if you can just stall Bexton as well as you did me," he muttered to himself, ignoring his passenger's outraged glare.

"Why are you stopping? We need to hurry!" Percival demanded as the duke pulled up his horses.

"That is why I'm stopping. Get off. You can take a hackney and follow."

"But—"

"I'm going to need all the speed I can get from my team. With two of us, it will slow them down," the duke explained curtly. He cracked the whip over his lead gelding's back sending him barreling through the London streets.

The Earl of Bexton quite complacently paced his team through the new mud of the country lanes. At least his delay had kept him out of the afternoon rain. This time being quite sober, the earl considered his proposed evening in pleasant anticipation. The little minx would doubtless be angry, at being tricked into coming, but Bexton was sure an extra crown or so would suitably soothe her.

Though the inn was rustic on the outside, the earl had a quite lavish private parlor and bedroom, and had ordered a fine repast to be awaiting them. And then, he had never really had trouble convincing females to enjoy his company, the earl thought smugly. Doubtless, her reticence before had but been on Stanford's account.

The earl's happy anticipation quickly changed as he spun into the old inn's courtyard to find the innkeeper nervously awaiting him. "Where's the hackney? I told you to have them wait?"

"I sent them up the road to search for the gel," the innkeeper advised unhappily.

"Search for her? What are you talking about?"

"I'm awful sorry, milord," the man shifted nervously. "It weren't none of our fault. She must 'ave just lit out through the rear door."

Bexton cursed. "I told you not to let the little wench out of your sight until I arrived."

"But milord, the gel, she acted 'appy as could be, once she learned who you were. Said she didn't mean no affront to you at the theater place. In fact, she couldn't wait to 'urry upstairs to get ready for you—fixed up and all."

"You bloody fool!" the earl snapped, easily guessing at Amber's strategy to get around the ignorant peasants. "Doubtless that blamed hackney coachman has lit out for London too." He sighed in exasperation. "Well, she will likely as not head back here, when she realizes there is not a thing between here and London but a lot of dark woods," Bexton said hopefully.

"I might as well let these beasts rest and at least enjoy some of the wine and food I sent out."

"Of course, my lord." The innkeeper quickly moved ahead of the earl to open the door for him. "I have a nice fire going in the private parlor, and will have your dinner right away."

It was but a few minutes later when the earl looked up, frowning at the clatter of hooves in the courtyard.

"Who the devil could that be coming here? Maybe that hackney did find her after all and brought her back?" he said hopefully.

"No," the innkeeper listened a moment. "Actually, it sounds more like someone is a goin' out of the courtyard."

"Going out? Oh, damn!" The earl leapt up to reach the door just in time to see his phaeton heading wildly toward the London road. "Your horse—where's your horse?" he demanded of the innkeeper.

"Horse? Well, I ain't got—"

"Your carriage then—anything. I have got to catch

that witch! If she gets to London with my team I shall never hear the end of it."

"Actually, all I have is my cart here, milord," the innkeeper advised anxiously "and it has—"

"Cart?" the earl shuddered. "Well, it shall have to do. Just hurry up and bring it about!"

"Yes, milord." The man headed to the rear of the inn at a trot.

The earl glanced briefly in the mirror considering his fine Bishop's blue waistcoat embroidered with peach roses and skin tight Jonquil unmentionables in distress. This was the first time he had even worn the new outfit and to have to ride in some farmer's cart—and on a muddy road at that. Heaven only knew how it would fair! Well, it had to be. He hurried out into the courtyard and stopped aghast. "What in Jove!"

"My cart, milord. All I 'ave is the donkey that pulls it. I was a tryin' to tell you."

The earl groaned. "Well, the stupid girl will doubtless run my beasts into a ditch the way she was driving them. No one can handle them but me, so I should not have to go far." He fastidiously brushed off the seat of the rickety two-wheeled cart with a lawn handkerchief before sitting down.

"Come on. Get up, now!" the earl found a bit of green sapling lying in the cart and raised it.

"Milord, don't—" the innkeeper shouted, but too late, as the whip came down.

The small donkey kicked out with both rear legs at the stinging whip, sending two huge wads of muddy detritus from the courtyard right onto the earl, before galloping wildly from the yard.

The innkeeper grimaced as the earl's curses could be heard long after the cart had vanished down the country lane.

* * *

Julian's brow was furrowed in intense concentration it took to hold his racing thoroughbreds on the narrow road. He should be nearing the inn. Julian slowed his team slightly on coming to a sharp corner.

"Good God!" The duke managed to swerve his team to the side as another vehicle flew right at him taking up the whole road.

Cecelia, not near so expert a handler, yanked back on the reins in panic at finding another carriage before her, sending the earl's phaeton into the ditch.

Julian pulled up his horses and ran back to where the wrecked vehicle lay canted against the muddy bank.

Julian's concern however turned to anger on seeing the driver sit up, apparently unharmed.

"You bloody idiot! What did you think you were—" The duke began but stopped as a shapely leg appeared over the side of the phaeton, followed by a flash of skirts.

Cecelia slid shakily down from the high perched seat. "J—Julian?" She blinked in shock at the man before her.

"Cecelia!" The duke rushed forward in relief. "Thank God! Are you all right?"

"I am not sure." She swayed, glad of the duke's support as his arms came about her. "I am terribly sorry. I fear I have never driven a team. I hope the horses are not injured?"

Julian glanced to where the pair stood trembling but unharmed. "They are all right. By Jove, is that not Bexton's rig?"

"I expect so. I took it from the inn yard," she said vaguely, holding her spinning head.

The duke's expression turned thunderous on remembering. "That bastard did not harm you?"

"No. Though his intent was obvious." Cecelia flushed in embarrassment. "But what are you doing here?" His form of address finally registered. "And you—you called me Cecelia?"

"Percival came to me when you were missing and explained everything. We shall speak of it later but for now I need to get you out of here."

Sweeping her up into his arms, the duke headed back to his own carriage.

"Julian, you do not have to carry me."

"You are still dizzy." The duke stopped at the angry voice coming down the road.

"You accursed beast, can't you move any faster?"

The duke stared in astonishment as a donkey cart came about the corner, its driver so covered in mud as to be unrecognizable.

"There's my phaeton!" Bexton grinned in satisfaction on seeing the wreck. "Now I've got you." The earl finally noticed the duke holding Cecelia. "What in the—? Stanford? By Jove, what are you doing here? But, I see you have caught the little doxy!"

"Bexton?"

"What? Oh!" The earl recalled his appearance in horror. "That thieving witch stole my phaeton, and this"—he muttered an expletive, pointing to the donkey—"was all I had to chase her in. And just look at what he's done to me!"

"Which is scarce more than you deserve, you—you unspeakable barbarian!" Cecelia's head was finally clearing. She made the duke set her down. "I shall have you thrown in the tower—"

"Me?" the earl snapped, climbing down from the farm cart. "I thoroughly intended paying you for the afternoon. But now it is I who shall have you thrown in the tower, you little—" He headed purposefully toward Cecelia only to find himself suddenly flying backwards into the mud when Julian's fist connected with his jaw.

"Stanford?" The earl shook his head to clear it, looking at the duke more in surprise than anger. "What in the blazes has gotten into you?" He struggled up.

"Keep your bloody distance!" the duke gritted. "You are just damned lucky she managed to get away from you unharmed!"

"Unharmed? I had no intention of hurting the wench—all I wanted was—" He staggered back in alarm at the duke's approach. "What the hell is wrong with you, Stanford! You said I was welcome to the wench when we were in White's but last evening! Now I suppose you have decided you want her after all?"

"What—is he talking about Julian?"

"I will explain later." The duke looked away from the pain in Cecelia's eyes. "Come, my dear." He reached for her hand but she backed away.

"You—you said he could—have me?"

"You don't understand, it wasn't—"

"Yes. I think I do understand! You are responsible for this man thinking it was perfectly all right to forcefully bring me out here to—to—" She couldn't manage the rest.

"My dear, it was not—" Julian reached for Cecelia's hand but she snatched it away.

"Your *dear*? Get away from me! I cannot believe I actually thought I had found a nobleman with some sense of decency!"

Just then, yet another vehicle came down the road from London.

The earl belatedly tried to hide behind Stanford as a hackney driver pulled up to the group. "Your Grace," the driver pulled at his cap, gaping at the others, "Lawd, that there's the Earl of Bexton, ain't it?"

Percival leaped from the carriage with a startled glance at the earl and donkey cart. "Sissy!" He ran to his cousin. "My dear, are you all right?"

"Oh Percy!" Cecelia ran into her cousin's arms. "Please take me away from here."

Chapter Fourteen

The tales spreading through a delighted ton about the earl's thwarted attempts to seduce a certain red-haired actress sent Bexton into ignominious hiding at his country seat. When that same actress vanished from London, most assumed Stanford had reclaimed his mistress and settled her somewhere near his own estate, though some snickered that Amber had scorned both the earl and duke, to go back north with her playwright.

As usual with the gossip mongers of the London society, no one came even close to the truth.

Lady Somersett forced a smile to cover the sudden pain when the couple before her moved apart in embarrassment.

"Cecelia." Constance self-consciously extricated herself from her husband's arms. "You are down early this morning."

"Yes, I just wished to hold your sweet little Elizabeth

before I leave." Cecelia crossed the bright morning room to a lacy bassinet.

"Leave?" Percival and Constance looked at one another in surprise. "But, Sissy, I thought you were staying through the summer?"

"Oh, heavens no. I have imposed on you for over two months now, it is quite time I return to tend to my own estate and allow you lovebirds some privacy in your new home." Cecelia's heart ached in longing when the baby tightened tiny fingers about her own. She gently hugged the little bundle, before handing her to her mother.

Constance was not in the least fooled by Cecelia's carefully controlled expression. "Oh Sissy, you should have babies of your own. Why don't you at least write the Duke of Stanford? It is quite apparent the man cares for you."

"I thought we were through discussing that subject?" Cecelia gave her cousin's wife a cool look. "But, as I have said before, he could have contacted me if he really wished to do so. I am certainly not writing when I have not heard a word from the man." She poured herself a cup of tea and sat down, assuming that ended the matter.

The practical minded Constance however only clucked in annoyance. "Cecelia, if you recall, you gave the duke such a complete dressing down before parting, he probably fears to write you. You could at least send the poor man a note to give him the option to apologize. After all, if you allow yourself to be honest, you know the whole situation was as much your fault as his."

"Perhaps, you ladies will excuse me." Percival rose in some alarm when Cecelia bridled.

"My fault?" Cecelia raised a brow archly, not even noticing her cousin's hasty departure. "That some

incorrigibly disgusting duke should be encouraged to assume he could—could—do what he wished with me—by giving me to another even more incorrigibly disgusting earl?''

"Well.'' Undaunted, Constance considered the matter a moment and then shrugged. "Yes. I am afraid it was quite your fault. After all Sissy, what do you expect the man to think when you are posing as an actress and my husband's mistress?''

"I do not think that I wish to discuss this.''

"Stanford did apologize to Percival,'' Constance ignored Cecelia's attempt to stop her, "and even admitted that he was just upset on thinking that you preferred Percival to him, when he told that earl that he could, well have you.''

"Constance!''

"Stanford said that last evening he understood you had agreed to be his mistress, but then—''

"I did no such thing!'' Cecelia sputtered in horror.

Constance again refused to be deterred. "Cecelia, I am only recounting what the duke told Percival. He said he had thought things settled between you and then you flung yourself back in your previous protector's arms right in front of him. Of course the poor man was upset.''

"I cannot believe Percival told you all of this!''

"Percy tells me everything. And the duke even went so far as to admit—''

"I will not listen to any more of this!'' Cecelia rose in anger.

"—that he had lost his heart to you even when he thought you but a cyprian!''

Cecelia stopped in the doorway. "He—he told Percy that?''

"I could scarcely know it otherwise.'' Constance

watched the other woman from under lowered lashes. "Percy also said how delighted the duke was to find you were truly a lady—though of course, I cannot imagine why that should have pleased the man so."

"Do you really suppose—" Cecelia began hopefully before catching herself. "Oh, this conversation is beyond ridiculous. I have packing to do."

"Sissy, I do wish you would reconsider and stay longer." Percival hugged his cousin while the last of her traps were loaded onto the coach.

"Thank you, Percy." Cecelia smiled. "I truly appreciate your hospitality in letting me stay so long."

"Letting you? My dear, we were quite delighted to have you. And after all you did for me! Why, I already have full bookings next season for my plays, so you shall have to come to London to see them."

"And I do hope you shan't still be angry at me by then so Lizzie and I can come stay with you?" Constance added anxiously.

Cecelia laughed. "You know very well you are impossible to remain angry with!" She warmly hugged Constance. "I do not know whether I shall go to London yet or not, but you and Percy are certainly welcome to the house whenever you wish."

"Now Cecelia," Percival looked at her in distress. "You quite promised me you were going to be the most avid supporter at my plays. I had so counted on you to subscribe to a box at the Barcelly, at the very least!"

"I don't know about the Barcelly," Cecelia demurred, trying to stifle memories a certain box at that theater brought to her. "Perhaps at Covent Garden, or one of the others. You did say your plays were going to be presented at several."

Percival's answer was stopped by the clatter of another carriage pulling up.

"Why Lady Somersett, you are not leaving?" Constance's mother stepped down from the old coach.

"Yes, I really must get back to my own estate, Mrs. Talley." Cecelia greeted the other woman pleasantly. "Did you and your family have an enjoyable trip?" Constance had advised her the family had spent a major portion of the summer at their older son's home.

"It was quite delightful. Edward has such a nice place in Edinburgh and the boys truly enjoyed the city. But I am still glad to get back. Oh, but why I came over—" Mrs. Talley reached into her reticule and withdrew two quite bedraggled letters and a third, fresher one. "I am so terribly embarrassed about this! These first two letters arrived for you before we left for our journey. I gave them to Mr. Talley to bring over, as he'd said he was coming to help Percival, and assuming he had given them to you, I quite put the matter from my mind. It was only on returning last week and finding yet another letter had arrived for you in our absence that I thought to ask Mr. Talley about the first ones. Would you believe that man had forgotten them? They were still in the pocket of his old hunting jacket!" She attempted to smooth the crumpled forms before handing them to Cecelia.

"Apparently, he had gotten caught in the rain on going over. He said he'd taken the wet coat off and tossed it over the saddle never once thinking of these letters. I do fear even the ink is quite run on them. Heaven knows if you shall even be able to decipher this mess, but at least the last one was not damaged."

It was with mixed feeling that Cecelia recognized the duke's bold handwriting on the three letters.

"They're from Stanford!" Constance cried excitedly

before realizing the significance of the delay in Cecelia
receiving them. "Oh dear! Mother, you said they
arrived—when?"

"Well, I don't quite recall. The first must have arrived
not long after you did, from London. And the last one,
that silly new maid said it came more than a month
ago. I asked why she didn't simply give it to Percival
when he came over to check on things, but she apparently just put it in with my post and forgot it. I am so
sorry, Lady Somersett. I do hope this has not caused a
problem?"

"Of course not, Mrs. Talley." Cecelia forced a smile.
"I am sure they were nothing important."

Cecelia feared to even read the letters in her reticule
and managed to avoid them for the first half of the
long-day's journey to Somersett. Finally, on re-entering
the carriage after a luncheon break, she drew them out.

"Dear Lady Somersett." Due to the way it was folded,
the first of the letter was still fairly legible. Cecelia could
read enough to discern a rather staid apology. Much as
he had told Percival, the duke had written a complete
and quite candid explanation of the happenings at his
club, this reference ended with, *"I can only hope you will
try to understand that when I told Lord Bexton you, or rather
'Amber' had 'returned to her playwright' it was without the
slightest suspicion that Philip might attempt to kidnap you. I
would never . . ."* The ink blurred at the bottom of the
sheet and she could read no further.

The top of the second sheet again was fairly clear, and
on it the duke proceeded with a quite mild chastisement
about the danger she had placed herself in by the unwise
manner of helping her cousin, but then after the missive's fold she could only make out "despite the impro-

priety of their relationship" and something about a "future meeting" though the words on either side were frustratingly lost.

Cecelia was somewhat encouraged by the signature, an elegantly scrawled Julian rather than just Stanford. Maybe the whole letter hadn't been just the obligatory apology.

With a bit more eagerness Cecelia opened the second, equally damaged communication. Smiling as it began more familiarly, *"My Dear Cecelia."* Again, the first fold of the letter was still readable. *"I can well imagine the shock of the situation with Bexton is what has restrained you from answering my prior communication. Please allow me to again assure you that I would never have purposely placed you in danger, whether as 'Amber' or the Lady Somersett". I shall never forgive myself for whatever careless words I spoke that evening that caused the man to . . ."*

Cecelia sighed heavily as the words again ran together from their long foray in Mr. Talley's pocket. The tone of this letter seemed much more personal, and the second page began expressing *"hopes that they might put all of that behind them"* but then the rest was lost. Cecelia tried desperately to make out anything from the remaining pages but could discern very little. At one point it almost appeared as though Julian had written of coming up there, she could decipher "hearing from you . . . post immediately to Cumbria . . ." and "My dar—" Was it possible that word had been "darling"? "Oh blast!" Cecelia tipped the thin paper about in the sunlight but the blurred ink gave her no further clues.

She brought out the third and last letter with grim foreboding for some minutes before forcing herself to break the seal. It was quite slim in relation to the others and being undamaged, unfortunately was easily read. He had reverted to the formal address of "Lady Somersett." His note quite succinctly allowed that quite obviously he had been mistaken in his previous assumptions, as she had refrained from even a note accepting his apologies. It had ended coldly that she could be assured he would not bother in writing further as her wishes were obvious. It was signed merely "Stanford."

Would he ever believe her if she told him what happened? Did she dare write back this late?

"My lady," Hannah worriedly counseled her downcast mistress some days later. "You must have started that letter a dozen times. Why ever don't you just tell His Grace you couldn't read his letters?"

"And you think he would believe it? Percival has heard from him and answered letters at the same address. And heaven knows, I've deceived Julian enough, he'd have good reason not to believe me." Cecelia morosely sighed. "He has doubtless taken such a disgust to me now for not even writing back that it's quite useless. Anyway, who's to say the notes were aught but an apology."

"I cannot imagine all that writing was simply an apology for that mess at the inn. You really must let him know what happened." At her mistress's sigh, Hannah shook her head. "Well at least just write accepting his apology, explain that you have been distraught, as an excuse for the delay."

"Oh, this is ridiculous." Cecelia abruptly rose, throwing her latest attempt at a letter to the duke in the trash receptacle. "I feel foolish writing something to a man I have not seen in three months. I have no idea how he perceives me. I cannot do this now. I believe I shall take the carriage over to visit the rector and his wife."

* * *

It was some days later when Cecelia finally completed
a note to Julian. She could not bring herself to explain
what had happened to his own letters, making them
unreadable. Their remaining in some squire's pocket
for three months sounded too incredible. Even if he
believed it, it would appear as though she were particularly anxious to know what the letters contained, which
of course, she was, but to let that be known to Julian
could be dreadfully embarrassing if they truly contained
naught of significance.

Cecelia's final letter revealed little of her true
thoughts and, in fact, was almost stilted. In it, she
allowed that the entire situation had been one she had
wished to put behind her as it was mentally distressing.
She did assure the duke that his apology was accepted
and offered her own for the "necessary deception" in
the matter of her posing as Amber. Cecelia added the
hopeful note that she would be at her house in London
for the holiday season, a decision she only made at that
moment, with the hope that he might call on her there.

The Duke of Stanford had penned his initial letters
in happy assurance that he had finally found the woman
he wished to make his duchess and that the lady cared
for him as he did for her. Though Cecelia had been
quite upset on their parting, Julian was confident once
her shock on the matter with Bexton was over, that she
would be more understanding.

He convinced himself it was quite all right to forgive
her for what he would normally have considered a fatal
breach of conduct for any lady. His darling just had

too kind a heart, that she should put herself into such jeopardy for her cousin.

The duke took Cecelia's initial reticence to answer his letter merely as further evidence of her embarrassment. Deciding perhaps he had not made his feelings clear enough, he sat down to pen a second letter. After some hesitation the duke chanced laying his heart before Cecelia, though having no real assurance of her own mind other than the feelings she had displayed as Amber. He awaited her reply quite anxiously.

The days turned into weeks without answer from the lady and the duke feared he had been precipitous, perhaps alarming her. But of course, that could be remedied with time, Julian consoled himself, recalling Amber's sweet response to being in his arms.

However, with the passage of more weeks without even a note acknowledging his avowal of love, the duke's humor darkened. Cecelia had doubtless just been amusing herself, using him to help that bloody Percival with his career! In wounded fury the duke determined he had had a narrow escape. With the woman's hoydenish behavior, how had he ever even considered her as an eligible Duchess of Stanford?

It was in that mood that he had written the final letter.

As the bright summer greens turned to wine tones of fall, Julian found himself totally out of sorts with his entire life. With little hope of pleasure, he sifted through the various invitations he received for the holidays.

"You do not intend entertaining at Stanford this year, Your Grace?" Barnstock inquired cautiously. His employer's mood had been testy for weeks.

"No." In the past, the duke had entertained at Stanford castle, inviting his married sisters to act as chatelaines, but this year he had no real enthusiasm for the season. "You may put the weekend of the fifteenth on my calendar, for the family dinner at Mother's," he advised the steward. "I will write an acceptance later." He set aside the dowager duchess's invitation for answer.

"Yes, sir." Barnstock made the notation and handed the duke several other letters. "It appears you have three invitations bearing the prince's seal."

Though most would kill for the honor of being included in "Prinny's" crowd, the duke grimaced. *Three?* I do not suppose I dare turn down more than one." He glanced through them and selected the evening of Christmas skits, and an afternoon function. "At least I can count on Levison's plays being entertaining. And may hope this luncheon shain't be as long as the dinner. On the dinner, make some excuse of a previous commitment."

Barnstock nodded. "And these, sir."

The duke flipped through a series of patently obvious invitations from other peerage with eligible, young daughters, handing them wordlessly back to Barnstock to decline.

"Hmm. Gantry said he will be spending the holidays at his hunting box outside London, and would enjoy a hunting companion." The duke read through the invitation in interest and finally handed it to his steward. "You may send my acceptances on this one. Tell Gantry, I shall be honored to spend the holidays with him. It is close enough to London that I can easily travel into town for those other functions."

"Excellent, sir." Barnstock smiled, pleased that the duke was finally exhibiting an interest in something.

* * *

Once his steward departed the library with the assignments, Julian penned a brief missive to his mother to be included with the steward's letters the next morning. That small duty finished, he poured himself a glass of claret and restlessly wandered over to sit before the fire, his thoughts, as they were often wont, turning to Cecelia, or more truthfully to Amber.

How many times he had dreamed of having his sweet Amber with him, just the two of them on a cold winter's eve before the fire. But Amber had never existed.

Amber was obviously naught but an act to keep his continued support for Lady Cecelia's beloved cousin. Doubtless, she had taken great amusement from her ability to keep his interest, while tantalizing him by holding her favors just out of reach.

The duke turned purposefully from his fire, perhaps that is what he needed. A real mistress. A warm and truly passionate woman to drive the memories of that cursed female from his mind. He would return to London and place some discreet inquiries.

Chapter Fifteen

"There is a letter for you, my lady," the housekeeper nodded to the packet on the tea tray she carried.

"A letter?" Cecelia quickly took it from the tray, but her heart sank on seeing Constance's handwriting.

Hannah watched expectantly as Cecelia opened the letter.

"It's just from the Levisons. I had written advising I might go to London for the holidays and invited them to join us."

Hannah took the tea tray from the elderly housekeeper and set it up before the fire. "Did they accept?"

"Yes, but here is some news," Cecelia smiled. "Would you believe, Constance said Percival has received an invitation, from no less than the prince himself, to put on a Christmas skit for the Carlton House festivities!"

"Oh my! That should truly seal Mr. Levisons's fortune, should it not? I just hope, that he isn't suggesting you play in these skits?"

"Heavens no," Cecelia laughed. "Daniel from *Justine,*

is continuing in Percy's plays this season. He has found Percy a new leading lady." She scanned the rest of the letter. "Apparently the duke recommended Percival's works to the prince, so at least Julian has not cast him off."

"Now my lady, His Grace has not had a chance to answer your letter. It has only been a bit over two weeks."

"It is now over three weeks Hannah. I am quite sure if he were going to answer, he would have." Cecelia sighed, having no way of knowing the duke had left his estate before her letter arrived. "But I am not going to think about that now. Constance is quite excited about Percival's prospects. She said he can get an invitation for me to go to Carlton House with them, if I'd like."

"To the prince's house! How exciting. You will go, will you not?"

"I should like to." Cecelia stirred sugar into her tea thoughtfully. "But I'm beginning to doubt the wisdom of even going to London."

"Something like this is just what you need to get your mind off that man," Hannah said impatiently.

"My mind is not *on* anyone!"

Hannah sighed, taking another tack. "Well, just imagine how much fun it would be to decorate Somersett House for Christmas. That curving staircase would be so lovely with holly flowing down it. You could set up a tree in the library and we could have a Yule log as well! Remember the stories you've told of your childhood Christmases there, how you loved them?"

"Yes, they were wonderful. My mother used to set up a tree and give a dance for the tenants," Cecelia reminisced. "You know with the extra money Percival gave me from the play and our harvest coming in so well, we might even be able to do something like that this year."

Hannah smiled contentedly as her mistress rambled on.

It was raining and quite cold when the Somersett carriage with Cecelia and Hannah drew up to the house in London some week and a half later.

"I'm glad you sent the staff ahead." Hannah shivered. "I am certainly ready for a warm fire."

"A spot of tea wouldn't be remiss either," Cecelia agreed. "What infernal weather."

"Isn't it? What is taking the coachman so long in fetching someone from the house?"

"Doubtless, Mrs. Walker is still trying to find the umbrellas," Cecelia laughed, pushing the door open. "Come on, we could be out here all night. I believe the rain has let up for a minute."

The two had no sooner stepped from the carriage than the light drizzle turned again into raging torrents.

"Why look, that carriage is stopping at the house down there. I do not recall seeing anyone residing there for ages." Lady Marion Leighmont pointed out to her older sister, the Viscountess Fulverton, their own carriage slowed by the storm. "Whose property is that anyway?"

"Some country baroness's—let's see," Emily considered, "Sumer's?—no—Somersett, that's it. Baroness Somersett. I believe her home is in the northern shires somewhere. Her parents and ours were friends, though I suppose you were too young to remember. I recall vaguely seeing the child the last time they were here. A tall gangly thing." She grimaced distastefully. "She must be into her twenties by now."

"I've never even heard of a Baroness Somersett."

"Small wonder. I've heard she's rather reclusive, seldom leaves her own estate. Never married I believe."

The two woman strained for a glimpse of the spinster as their carriage edged closer. Two bundled figures hurried from the other equipage. "Hmm. The baroness is in her twenties, you say?" Marion asked thoughtfully. "And never married? Doubtless she must be a quiz, but you know, Sister, this just might be the answer to our little problem."

The other woman looked at her blankly.

"For dear cousin Melville?" Marion prompted. "A dinner partner?"

"But that is tomorrow evening. No one would accept an invitation this late."

"Except perhaps some long-in-the-tooth spinster—just in from the country?" Marion replied slyly.

Emily laughed. "For shame, Marion! But with a dinner partner to attend to, dear Melville would not be able to corner the duke with those boring estate problems."

"Exactly," Emily said smugly, "and Stanford will be free to better acquaint himself with my dear Amanda!"

"And my Lillian," Marion added with a cool glance. "Just imagine, my sweet baby, a duchess!"

"I'd prefer to imagine her a cousin to one! But we had best see this woman first. We do not want to risk inviting another female who might detract from our own daughters." Emily considered for a moment. "Why don't we stop by now?"

"But the baroness has only just arrived. That would scarcely be proper."

"Well, we do not know for *certain* that she just arrived, now do we?"

Marion smiled in understanding. "You are right, of

course, Sister. And the poor dear will probably be beside herself at receiving an invitation into society so soon.''

Cecelia laughed, surveying herself in the hall mirror. ''Heavens, I look much like the proverbial drowned rat!''

'' 'The rain has lightened'—indeed!'' Hannah removed her own sodden coat. ''But at least this kept me fairly dry. Your dress is soaked, my lady. We had best get you upstairs and into something dry.''

''I am terribly sorry, Lady Somersett,'' Mrs. Walker, the housekeeper, apologized, ''but I fear the fires are not lit yet in your rooms. We hadn't expected you until later. I've only just now sent Bridget up with a scuttle, so it might be best if you stay by the parlor fire until your room has time to get warm.''

''That is a good idea.'' Cecelia stifled a shiver.

''Oh dear, my lady, you are soaked to the skin.'' The housekeeper worried. ''Heaven knows how long it will be before they get your carriage unpacked. But wait— I think I have something—''

The woman rushed from the room to return with an outdated brown cloak. ''This was in one of the wardrobes upstairs, miss. I don't know who it belonged to, but at least it is warm and dry.''

''Warm and dry sounds wonderful right now.'' Cecelia laughed, wrapping the cloak gratefully about her. ''Now if I can just stop this mass of hair from dripping down my back—'' Cecelia pulled her long thick hair from its ruined coiffure. After drying most of the water from it, she wrapped it into a tight bun. She was just pinning it atop her head when the butler appeared at the parlor door.

"You have callers, my lady."

"Callers? In this weather?" Cecelia frowned. "Well, I certainly cannot see anyone now, just tell them to leave cards." She stopped in shock when two elegant ladies stepped into the parlor.

"Oh, I am chilled to the bone!" Emily said gaily, by way of excusing herself for pushing past the butler. "Perhaps we can await by the fire while you take our cards to your lady?"

On seeing Cecelia, Lady Leighmont acted quite surprised. "Oh my, I didn't realize anyone was in here. Please forgive us, Lady Somersett."

Cecelia could scarce demand they leave at that stage and had to make the best of the matter. "Not at all. Do come in." She glanced at the cards the butler handed her. "Lady Leighmont. Lady Fulverton. I fear I have only just arrived from my country estate, and my abigail and I quite got caught in the storm on entering."

"You poor dear!" Marion allowed with a satisfied glance at her sister. The baroness was everything they had hoped. "We had no idea you had just now taken up residence. I told my dear sister that I saw lights in your home the other night. We were so excited to meet you that we had to quite force ourselves to wait until today to come by," the viscountess said chattily. "You may not recall, but I was a friend of your dear mother's."

Cecelia managed an appropriate murmur.

"Now Lady Somersett, we shall not keep you as I see we are quite inopportune," Emily joined in brightly, "but we came by especially to invite you to our dinner party tomorrow evening."

Cecelia tried to decline but the woman would have none of it. "Several of your parents' friends shall be there, and they are all so eager to meet you. I pray you shan't deny me?''

Once back in their carriage, the two ladies congratulated themselves on their successful ploy. ''My, the poor dear—no looks or style at all. Could you believe that hair?'' Emily shuddered delicately. ''I do believe she is even more gauche than she was as a child.''

''Let us hope she has something reasonably suitable to wear for dinner,'' Marion worried aloud. ''Our guests are rather influential, you know. Could you believe that dreadful cloak she had on? I was quite embarrassed for her. And that parlor! It almost appeared as though it had been stripped.''

''Such a pity. She's probably having to sell things to live. Well, at least, we needn't have any concern about her catching the duke's eye.''

The following day Cecelia flung herself into refurbishing Somersett House. ''I simply must get to the linen drapers this morning,'' she advised Hannah. ''I had all but forgotten about stripping the parlor for that house Percival let for Amber.''

''But my lady, I thought you brought all those items back the day we were to leave from the place.'' Hannah had never heard the whole of the story.

''I started to bring them back, but that is when I was abducted by that Bexton fiend's men. I gave the box of linens to those ruffians to distract them while I slipped away.''

''Oh dear, my lady, I never knew—'' Hannah began in distress.

''But that is all past.'' Cecelia waved Hannah's concern aside. "I needed to refurbish this parlor anyway. Tomorrow we will go shopping. I think I will stop by Bond Street and purchase a new gown for that dinner party as well. Maybe that will make it worth letting myself get forced into accepting the invitation."

Chapter Sixteen

"Oh, my lady, you truly look lovely!" Hannah sighed, buttoning the last tiny pearls up the back of Cecelia's rose silk dinner dress.

"Thank you, Hannah. I must admit Lady Leighmont's note this morning, advising me on the manner of dress for dinner, quite put my nose out of joint! Otherwise I should never had bought something quite so elegant."

Hannah chuckled, putting the finishing touches on her mistress's sleek blond coiffure. "You can scarcely blame those two for their opinion considering how you looked from that storm. And with the parlor stripped like that, they doubtless assumed you were quite under the hatches."

"I admit I have been close to the gullgropers, but fortunately Somersett's finances are now somewhat repaired, thanks to Percival." She glanced at the ormolu clock on the mantel. "Well, I suppose it is time to go, though I fear this evening shall be a dreadful bore."

* * *

"I am truly sorry, Stanford," the viscount apologized, at the duke's expression on entering their home. "I had no idea Emily had turned our dinner into a social event until I came down myself this evening."

"It is no matter, Fulverton." Julian's gaze dismally surveying the crowded parlor, belied the obligatory politeness.

"Your Grace, what a delight to see you again!" The viscount groaned inwardly when his wife immediately intercepted the duke, their young daughter in tow. "You do recall our dear little Amanda? Well, not so little anymore"—she gave a tinkling laugh—"in fact my Amanda is quite the young lady now, do you not agree?"

"Miss Fulverton." Forcing a smile, the duke bent over the blushing girl's hand.

"It seems but yesterday that this sweet child was in the schoolroom, and now here she is, already of a marriageable age."

"My dear," the viscount said at the duke's darkening countenance. "Why don't you take Amanda to see Lord and Lady Whitson over there. Albert just mentioned yesterday how long it had been since he had seen the child."

Ignoring his wife's covert glare, Fulverton led the duke toward his library. "Perhaps if we retire somewhere quieter—"

"Why Lord Fulverton!" Julian was almost amused at the viscount's harassed expression when his sister-in-law, Lady Leighmont sailed across the room toward them, her own young debutante eagerly following. "I don't believe I have had a chance to speak to you this evening." She smiled with a flirtatious glance up at the duke. "And I do not believe the duke has ever met your niece."

Forced into the introduction, Charles Fulverton avoided Julian's eyes. "Stanford, may I present Miss Leighmont. Lillian, His Grace, the Duke of Stanford."

Fulverton had barely finished that introduction when Julian noticed the dowager Countess Blackwood heading in their direction. Knowing her as one of the worse gossip mongers in the ton, the duke had no intention of getting caught in one of her interrogations. He looked across the room. "I do believe that is your cousin Melville, is it not, Fulverton? I am sure he is waiting for us. You will excuse us, my lady, Miss Leighmont?"

"You are a lot better at that than I am." Charles chuckled when he and the duke were safely away from the disappointed women.

"I have had a lot of practice," Stanford allowed dryly. "Now I pray that one of these gentlemen truly is your cousin."

"Fortunately. The tall thin young man by the fireplace. Come, I'll introduce you."

The three gentlemen were engaged in conversation and paid no attention when the butler announced a late arrival.

"Lady Cecelia Somersett."

"Excellent, the woman arrived just in time," the viscountess said *sotto voce* to her sister. "Now we can get Melville away from the duke." She turned to greet her guest.

"Lady Fulverton. Lady Leighmont." Cecelia came over to the two staring women. "I do apologize for being so late."

"Oh—of course." Emily was unsuccessful in hiding her dismay at the sight of the strikingly beautiful woman. "Why, my dear, what a—lovely gown."

"Thank you." Cecelia leaned closer with a conspiring smile. "And I must thank you also for your kindness in sending me that note. I should never have thought to purchase a new gown otherwise!"

Marion gave her sister a dark look.

"Yes, well uh, let me introduce you to my dear cousin Melville. He has been so eager to meet you."

The women hurriedly escorted Cecelia through the staring guests. "Harold, I must introduce you to my dear friend, Lady Cecelia Somersett."

The duke spun in disbelief at the name.

"Julian! What—" Cecelia stammered in shock on finding herself staring up into the familiar cool eyes.

"You—know each other?" Emily asked in surprise.

"Yes." Stanford was the first to recover. His anger at Cecelia perversely flared at finding her more lovely than he had even imagined. "Lady Somersett, an—unexpected surprise." His tone clearly implied it was also an unpleasant one.

Cecelia's face burned in embarrassment when with but a brief nod of acknowledgment to her stammered greeting, the duke turned pointedly back to Fulverton. "Perhaps we might finish our conversation in your library, Charles?"

"Uh, Lady Somersett," the young Melville was aghast at the duke's treatment of Cecelia, "I am so pleased to meet you. Lady Fulverton said our parents were friends I believe."

Cecelia managed a grateful smile, allowing the young man to continue a monologue until she had her composure back enough to join in his conversation.

At dinner Cecelia was relieved to find she and Harold were seated at maximum distance from the more elite guests. The two young daughters of the family were, for obvious reasons, seated near the duke.

Though she tried not to care, watching the duke encouraging the two girls' silly banter merely sunk her into deeper depression. It was obvious Julian had changed his mind about the marriage mart. Doubtless the two delightful young debutantes of the family were the reason he had chosen to attend the function.

"Did you say your estate is in Cumbria?" Mr. Melville noticed Cecelia's taut features and sought to distract her.

"Yes, in the south." Cecelia turned her attention to the young man, and was surprised to find him quite knowledgeable on her region.

"Your estate must have suffered from the flooding last year as well. That is what I've come to discuss with my cousin and the duke as they've had the same problems, though in a different area."

"Is that why the duke came tonight?"

She regretted the question at the man's sympathetic smile. "I couldn't say, but as to your flooding, was it severe last spring? I know several estates quite lost their first crops."

"And mine was one. I had to subsidize the crofters to keep them in food until the second planting could come up. I only pray that the autumn does not bring a repeat."

"If I may be so bold, I have had a bit of experience in the lowland farms in your area. For instance, at the Dalhamer Estate I found a series of low dikes combined with trenches solved the earl's problem, both of flooding and irrigation in the dry season."

"That was your idea? I heard the earl had resolved

his own flooding and wondered how." Cecelia soon was quite engrossed in the young man's ideas.

The duke glanced covertly down the table at Cecelia. For all appearances she had totally forgotten his presence and was engaged in some involved discussion with young Melville. For a reason he refused to admit, her laughter at something Melville said, quite rankled His Grace.

After dinner the guests trooped resolutely into the music room where the two girls proudly displayed their musical accomplishments. Both of the girls' mothers were encouraged by Stanford's apparent rapt attention when they sang, little knowing his thoughts were on a very different soprano.

At one point, Cecelia risked a shuttered glance at the duke. She was surprised to find him watching her, an few oddly poignant look in his eyes. Their gaze met for a few long seconds before Cecelia colored and looked away.

The aging Countess Blackwood raised her brows at the look she had caught between Cecelia and the duke. The girl had certainly reacted strongly to seeing the duke—and then there was the way the duke had totally cut the baroness. That was certainly not like Stanford. He was known to be quite one of the more polite gentlemen of the ton. Lady Somersett would have had to do something extremely untoward for Stanford to treat her like that. The countess smiled to herself. It might prove interesting to keep an eye on those two.

Cecelia decided she'd endured all she could for the evening when the guests reconvened in the parlor. She offered her excuses to Mr. Melville. "I have enjoyed our discussion, sir, but I fear I am yet weary from my journey."

"I have doubtless quite bored you with all this talk of agronomy."

"No, not at all, Mr. Melville. In fact, I have been wondering if I might be so bold as to bespeak your services? That is, if you plan on being in my shire some time in the future?"

Melville smiled in pleasure. "My dear lady, I should be quite honored. Actually, I expect to proceed to the Earl of Galloway's estate right after Michaelmas, which is but a bit north of you. If it is convenient, I would be delighted to stop by your estate then?"

The duke caught just enough of the couple's conversation over the twittering of the two girls at his side, to bring a scowl to his handsome features. Refusing to admit jealousy to himself, the duke decided his irritability was merely on having to be exposed to Lady Somersett's perfidy yet again.

After finalizing Mr. Melville's future visit, Cecelia approached the viscountess with her apologies for leaving early. "I have enjoyed the evening, Lady Fulverton, but I find I am yet quite weary from my journey from Cumbria."

"Of course, you poor dear. I shall have my butler call your carriage around." Emily was more than a little relieved to have the baroness depart early. She too had noticed the looks between the duke and Cecelia.

Emily however had not anticipated that the duke would follow Cecelia's early exit.

"But, Your Grace"—the viscountess tried unsuccessfully—"I had thought you wished to discuss some matters with my husband and young Melville?"

"We have already arranged to meet at my club later in the week." Julian smiled wryly at her belated recalling of the real purpose of his visit.

"May I speak with you a moment, Lady Somersett?"

The duke stopped Cecelia just as she went to step into her carriage.

Cecelia hesitated briefly before nodding to her groom to wait. "Of course." She carefully tried to hide her emotions when Julian led her a brief distance from the carriage.

"I had not expected you to be here tonight," Julian said curtly, "or I should have declined the invitation. Since you disdained to accept my apology for past events, I am certain you would welcome further such unexpected encounters even less than myself: Perhaps we can come upon some plan to avoid one another in the future?"

The Countess Blackwood listening from the darkened verandah, scarcely contained her excitement. She had been right, there *was* something going on between these two!

"Julian." Cecelia tried unsuccessfully to hide the pain of her voice. "I cannot fault you for your disgust of me. Though I know it was quite belated, I did write accepting your apology, and offering my own. I realize now that all the things that led up to that—unfortunate matter at the inn were my own fault. I had no right to condemn you for acting toward me as I myself had led you to consider appropriate."

The duke was momentarily stunned by her painful confession. "What do you mean you accepted my apology? Cecelia, I have not received any letter from you." He looked up, cursing softly as someone came out for their carriage.

"But I wrote to you."

The duke shushed her. "We had best go now before someone sees us, but I have to speak to you. May I call on you, tomorrow?"

"Of course." Cecelia's hopes were raised. "I am at Somersett House."

"No, I'm sorry. I can not come tomorrow," the duke recalled. "I had forgotten I have a commitment to be out of town." He had accepted an invitation to hunt with Gantry the next morning and could not gracefully back out this late. "May I come Friday morning?"

After settling on a time, the two departed to their own carriages.

Neither noticed the countess gleefully slipping back inside the house.

Chapter Seventeen

"The Duke of Stanford was at Lady Fulverton's!" Hannah repeated in excitement.

"Yes, but don't come up with some maggoty notion." Cecelia tried to keep her own hope from showing. "Actually, Julian quite gave me the cut direct at first."

"But you said—"

"Yes, I'm getting there. As I was leaving, Julian did approach me. His initial purpose was to avoid attending the same functions again, but then . . ." Cecelia related their brief conversation.

Hannah sighed in relief. "So you finally told the poor man you hadn't been able to read his letters?"

"Well, no, not exactly." Cecelia ignored her maid's exasperated look. "But I did tell him I had written. Apparently, he left his own estate before receiving my letter."

"Well, I'm glad you at least told him that much! So His Grace will be here tomorrow?" Hannah continued happily, despite her mistress's quelling glance on her prior comment. "We must finish the parlor today then and—" she looked at Cecelia critically. "Let's see, your green cambric? No, that new cream with the red satin stripe you purchased was to be ready today! I'll have Mrs. Walker send one of the maids over for it this morning. Red will be perfect for the holidays. Now we must decide on your hair. I do believe I've some velvet ribbon . . ."

Cecelia allowed herself to fall in with Hannah's optimistic mood.

The Duke of Stanford's excellent humor was remarked on during the hunt at Gantry. Before leaving London, Julian had dispatched a messenger to fetch Cecelia's letter from Stanford, confident that its contents would finally acknowledge his stated love.

"Well, that was quite a jolly chase, even though the wily little rascal evaded us, don't you think, Stanford?" Gantry led the younger man into his library, where the hunters were gathering.

"It was an excellent hunt," Julian agreed. "If I may dare, I admit I prefer not killing the fox anyway. It has always seemed a shame to destroy a beast which gives such an enjoyable chase."

"True. Not to mention it is an unworthy payment to demand for such a small bit of brush," the earl quipped with a mischievous glance.

Julian chuckled, accepting a glass of port from the circulating servants. "It was indeed a pleasure riding out with you again, Gantry. I recall so many fond times in my boyhood." The two men contentedly engaged in reminiscences, little knowing the gossip that was being spread by the late arriving guests from London.

During dinner, the duke engaged in an interesting

discussion with Gantry on reports received from Castlereigh in Vienna, never noticing the covert glances he was receiving from the female members of the dinner party. It was only when he obligingly turned from the more interesting discussion to the young matron sitting on his left, that the duke realized something was afoot.

"Lady Bainbridge, may I say you look quite charming tonight?" The duke attempted to open a polite conversation.

"Thank you, Your Grace," the woman responded coolly and turned away.

Julian raised a questioning brow at Gantry.

The earl merely shrugged. "A newly wedded chit," he excused in an amused undertone before continuing the preceding conversation on the Vienna Congress.

Yet curious about the woman's odd reaction, Julian began paying more attention to the other dinner guests' conversations. It took little time to realize his name was on every tongue.

"It appears you are the prime *on-dit* of the evening," the earl acknowledged to Julian a few minutes later. "Any idea what it's about?"

Julian grimaced cynically. "With the ton, who knows? The only thing I can think of is that word might have gotten out that I've been checking the muslin market."

"You are looking for another mistress? What became of that actress? I heard you'd taken her away from Bexton again and set her up in the country somewhere."

Julian gave his friend a cool look. "Amber never belonged to Bexton. And, she was not in my keeping."

The earl shrugged. "Well, if you are in the market, I heard there is a delightful new *fille de joie* from Paris at the—"

"Thank you, but I have since changed my mind in that regard," Julian interrupted. "And perhaps it would give me some respite from the gapers if you allow us to leave the table, my friend?''

The earl realized belatedly his guests had all finished their meal. ''Oh, of course.'' He set his own glass down and rose.

A slightly foxed young lord stopped Julian on exiting the dining hall. ''Well, Stanford, I hear congratulations are in order—or is it condolences?''

Julian gave the man a cold look. ''Balfour, I haven't the faintest notion what you are prattling about!''

''Then you are the only one in the room that doesn't know,'' the young man chortled.

''Then perhaps you will be so good as to tell me, just *what* it is that I don't know?''

''Come, old man, it happens to the best of us. At least I hear she's a diamond of the first water. The Baroness Somersett, is it? I don't think I've met the lady.''

Julian felt a chill of apprehension. ''People are talking about Lady Somersett and me?''

Balfour looked at him in disbelief. ''Surely, you know it is all over London, your rendezvous at the inn with the baroness?''

''My what?''

''You can't intend to deny it, Stanford. The woman's ruined.''

Julian abruptly yanked Balfour to the side. ''What in the hell are you talking about?''

''Now I did not mean anything, Your Grace.''

''Just tell me what is being said!''

''Well, uh, the Countess Blackwood apparently overheard the two of you at some dinner party. She said the lady in question was practically begging your forgiveness for her indiscretions at some inn.''

''Good God!'' The duke suddenly realized what had

happened. In dismay, he recalled Cecelia's words. "That damned meddling marplot."

He had to get back to London immediately before Cecelia found out about any of this. "Give Gantry my excuses, Balfour."

Julian was out the side door before the man could reply.

Julian chastised himself the entire way back to London. How could he have been so foolish as to accost Cecelia where anyone could hear! It was his own confounded jealously of that Melville chap, that had led to this. On retrospect, it was only too clear how her painful apology to him would have sounded to that damn gossip-hungry eavesdropper!

With any luck, Cecelia might not have heard the rumors. The duke sprang his horses, scarcely able to bear the thought of Cecelia being subjected to the humiliation of what was being spread about by the ton.

If he could just reach Cecelia and propose before she heard anything. The special license was no problem, with his connections. He would take her off to Stanford immediately. They could be wed there, in his own chapel by the sea. Even the most intrepid gossips would not dare say anything about the Duchess of Stanford!

Julian smiled to himself as visions of fireside evenings with his love once again accompanied his mind.

"What?" Hannah listened in horror to what the young maid had heard whispered about in the vegetable market that morning. "Oh heavens! Don't you dare breathe a word of this to anyone, unless you wish yourself to be on the street,'' she threatened before taking her mistress's tea tray up to her.

"Is there a note from Julian?'' Cecelia asked nervously, over her breakfast tray. "He was not sure when he could come by.''

"No, my lady.'' Hannah carefully kept her face turned. "But if I were you, I shouldn't dawdle over my scones, in case he comes early.'' Surely, the duke would have heard the rumors, and would protect Cecelia. Hannah frowned, that is, unless she was wrong about the man's feelings!

"Lady Somersett.'' Mrs. Walker tapped on the door a few minutes later. "His Grace, the Duke of Stanford, is below for you.'' She glanced at Cecelia's dressing gown. "Shall I advise him you are indisposed?''

"No!'' The housekeeper's eyebrows rose in surprise at Hannah's answering for Cecelia. "Lady Somersett is expecting the duke. Tell him she'll be but a minute.''

"Heavens I really was not expecting the man this early.'' Cecelia laughed, setting aside her breakfast tray.

"The earlier, the better,'' Hannah muttered, hurrying to the wardrobe.

"What?''

"Nothing, miss.'' Hannah fetched her gown. "Just slip into this and I'll have you ready in a minute.''

Julian stared moodily out the parlor window, ignoring the tea tray brought by Cecelia's housekeeper. His good humor of the previous evening had been dashed with the morning's mail.

Cecelia's letter was in the packet.

Julian had opened it in eager anticipation, but rather than the hoped for reaction to his declaration of love, he had been dismayed to find only a very brief note accepting his apology and offering her own. Cecelia had made no reference at all to anything in his letters, except the apology.

Julian had read the brief missive over, at first in disbelief, and then in growing distress. The woman had simply ignored the quite plain message of his letters. That left him with only one conclusion. That his avowal of love had been unwelcome.

This time the duke could not even manage to engender any anger at Cecelia to cover his own pain. She simply did not love him. But she would have to marry him or live her life shunned by even the least of the peerage!

Julian's intention had been to try to keep the rumors from Cecelia, but after reading her letter, he knew the only way he could ascertain that she would marry him, was to tell her of them.

The duke drew in his breath at her loveliness when Cecelia came into the room.

"Good morning, Your Grace." Cecelia tried to hide her nervous anticipation behind the formal greeting. "I apologize for keeping you waiting. I had not expected you so early."

The duke found what he had to say extremely difficult under the circumstances. Last night he had envisioned taking Cecelia in his arms and declaring his love, but now even her stilted greeting bespoke of her lack of feeling for him.

"Forgive me, for disturbing your morning." With difficulty the duke kept his own tone cool, impersonal. "But I'm afraid it was necessary."

Cecelia's face paled at his grim countenance. "Julian, is something wrong?"

The duke hesitated but a moment, "Yes, I'm afraid there is."

* * *

Hannah stopped her impatient pacing of the hallway to quickly open a convenient drawer when the duke came from the parlor. Her subversive actions were unnecessary since he seemed not to even notice her. Julian strode out the door scarcely giving the butler time to hand him his coat.

Hannah felt her heart sink. Surely, her foolish mistress had not refused the man?

Hannah barely waited for the front door to close behind the duke before she rushed into the parlor.

The abigail stopped in alarm at finding her mistress sitting quite pale and stiff on the settee.

"Oh dear! He didn't tell you?" Hannah blurted out without thinking.

"You knew?"

Hannah nodded. "I'm sorry, my lady."

"Oh God. I suppose that means those horrid rumors are all over London." Cecelia's voice broke in distress.

"Don't you let it upset you now." Hannah came over to Cecelia anxiously. "What did His Grace say?"

"He—he said he would—marry me. He's getting a special license this morning."

Hannah laughed in relief. "Well, then, congratulations, my lady! And I don't think the new Duchess of Stanford is going to have to worry about anyone daring to spread rumors."

"Oh Hannah." Cecelia's eyes filled with tears. "You don't understand! Julian didn't ask me to marry him because he wants to, but because he feels he has to, to save my reputation."

"Oh fustian!" Hannah dismissed. "The man's been besotted of you ever since he first saw you as Amber."

"But he only wanted me as his mistress!" Cecelia looked away.

"My lady," Hannah tried to keep the impatience from her voice, "what *else* could a duke ask of an actress? Especially one presumably in the keeping of another man! And the duke pursued his interest in you even after he knew you were a peeress, totally ignoring convention! Surely this proves the strength of his feelings?"

"Or that he felt honor bound to do the noble thing, even then!" Cecelia added wryly, accepting the handkerchief Hannah offered. "Hannah, it was so mortifying when he told me! I could scarcely even speak. To think of the entire ton out there whispering how I and Julian—"

"There now." Hannah tried to calm her. "The ton is always talking about something. You know very well this shall all blow over as soon as the gossip mongers latch onto some other poor hapless soul to discredit. And after all, my lady, it is nothing more than they thought of you as Amber." Hannah's reasoning was logical but unwise.

"Hannah! How could you say such!"

"But my lady, you *were* posing as Mr. Levison's mistress and then even the duke's."

"That was altogether different! Amber was an actress! It was quite expected that the gentry should assume she would do such. But this is about *me!*"

Hannah considered Cecelia's statement in some confusion before deciding to bypass it. "My lady, I believe what you need to do is simply put all of those rumors from your mind. You have said the duke is procuring a special license."

"Yes. That is where he went, just now."

"Then we haven't long to plan for your wedding! Did he mention the arrangements?"

"He wishes for us to be married in his chapel at Stanford, this very evening," Cecelia declared morosely. "He said he has already sent out messages to have everything in order."

Hannah smiled to herself. Her mistress had obviously accepted the man. Hannah was quite sure Cecelia would never have agreed to marry the duke if she didn't really love him, regardless of the circumstances. And the duke, Hannah was equally certain, could have found some way out of the predicament had *he* truly wished to do so. Doubtless, after their wedding night, neither of them would care a whit for the rumors, but that was scarcely something the abigail could tell her young mistress.

"Come, my lady. Why don't we go upstairs and decide what you shall take to Stanford?"

Chapter Eighteen

The plush brougham Julian had dispatched for Cecelia rolled through acres of groomed carriageway even after passing the huge stone portals heralding the beginnings of Stanford.

"The duke's estate must be dreadfully large," Hannah commented idly.

She glanced over in concern when Cecelia remained silent like she had most of the trip. "My lady, are you all right?"

"I suppose," Cecelia pulled herself from her thoughts. "Do you think Julian shall already be here?"

"I should imagine so. He did leave out some three hours before us. Oh look, my lady, the castle towers are in view!"

Cecelia's mood was lifted briefly by the three graceful spires rising above the trees on the hilltop ahead. "Stanford must be right on the ocean's side."

"Yes, I do believe I can even smell the sea!" Hannah

said appreciatively. "It shall be much like living at Somersett."

Cecelia turned from the window. "Hannah, I do not expect that we shall be residing at Stanford for very long."

"The duke has some other residence he prefers?"

"No." Cecelia took a careful breath. "Julian and I, as you know, had another discussion before he departed."

"My lady?" Hannah looked at her mistress's pale features in dread. She had not liked either of their demeanors on exiting from that brief second meeting. "Surely you are not considering changing your mind about marrying him?"

"I fear, at this point, marriage is unavoidable." Cecelia's tone was emotionless. "I would be totally ruined and even Julian has allowed he should not be pleased with having such a stigma attached to his name."

"Then, why did you say we shall not be at Stanford long?" Hannah asked carefully.

"The duke advised me that he has considerable power at court. He said that if I wished, he could arrange to have the marriage quietly annulled after a time and—"

"Oh no!" Hannah interrupted Cecelia in horror. "You didn't! Surely, you didn't tell the poor man that's what you wished?"

"I am certain Julian would not have even suggested such were it not in hopes that I would agree. Now, I just wanted to warn you but I don't wish to discuss the matter further."

Hannah groaned, barely stifling the urge to give her mistress a good shaking. Were the gentry *always* so incredibly birdwitted!

And only this morning she had such an encouraging

talk with Alvin! When the duke's coachman had been
so pleased that Hannah would be residing at the estate
with her mistress, the abigail had entertained hopes of
perhaps a husband for herself as well as Lady Cecelia.

The duke's extensive staff were lined up before the
castle entrance when the carriage pulled up.

Cecelia could scarcely bear her mixed emotions. The
castle was so incredibly lovely and Julian, awaiting her,
so incredibly handsome.

"Welcome, my dear." The duke's voice showed none
of his own pain when he opened the carriage door for
Cecelia.

Cecelia was not encouraged by his presence. Julian
had explained the necessity of having the marriage
appear outwardly normal.

"Thank you." She accepted the duke's hand to step
down from the carriage, though carefully avoiding his
eyes.

Cecelia felt like weeping, when she smilingly greeted
each of the happy servants. She could not have imagined
a home nor a man so close to her secret dreams. Why
had it all gone so wrong?

The entire castle sparkled in readiness for its new
mistress with flowers gracing every room. Cecelia could
scarcely believe how much the duke had accomplished
in such a short period.

Even her chambers next to the duke's appeared to
have been quite recently renewed, though of course
that was impossible. Cecelia smiled at the graceful hang-
ings of rose, draped about a delicate poster bed. Deep
silk curtains looped back from tall mullioned windows
overlooking the ocean, again in her favorite shade of
rose. It was almost as though it had been refurbished
especially for her.

"My, look at this room. Why these chambers might

have been redone just with you in mind." Hannah voiced Cecelia's thoughts aloud, neither knowing that was precisely what the duke had done, after writing his first optimistic letter to Cecelia.

"I imagine the duke's mother must have preferred the same colors as I," Cecelia discounted. "Obviously the duke had no time to redecorate."

She could not, however, restrain her pleasure at the flowers bedecking the rooms. Vase upon vase of *elegante* roses, her very favorite flower, lent their sweetness to the balmy ocean breeze entering the open windows. Could the duke really have mentioned her love for those particular roses to the housekeeper, or had the woman selected them just because the color went so well with the room?

"My lady, we must get you dressed," Hannah quietly reminded Cecelia.

Cecelia drew in her breath on entering the castle's chapel. The small sanctuary encompassed the ground floor of the seaside tower. The chapel's long stained glass windows, bathed the ancient room in beautiful streams of color from the setting sun.

The perfume of roses again fragranced the rarefied air of the old church.

"It is beautiful," Cecelia breathed in wonder, momentarily forgetting her despair when the duke came up beside her.

"Thank you." Julian forcefully drew his eyes from the even greater beauty of the woman at his side. "I arranged for a simple ceremony. Under the circumstances, I did not wish to submit you to more than necessary."

Unable to speak, Cecelia just nodded when he took her hand and tucked it over his arm.

Cecelia was glad the duke's staff did not know the real reason for her misty eyes when Julian led her past them to the altar. She took an odd comfort in the aged Stanford vicar's encouraging smile, when they knelt before him.

Cecelia had feared she might not be able to manage the sacred marriage vows to this man who didn't really love her. But when the vicar recited that holiest of ceremonies, Cecelia knew, at least for her, the vows were very real. She loved Julian, and was truly giving her heart to this man.

The duke too, realized he spoke but the truth when he vowed to love and cherish the woman beside him. And though he had previously offered to let Cecelia go, Julian silently made another vow—to do everything possible to convince her to stay.

With renewed determination to win his bride's heart, the duke set about putting Cecelia at ease during their wedding supper.

"I had thought perhaps on the morrow I might show you a bit of the estate," the duke offered, to remove both their minds from the impossibility of the coming night. "I have a sweet paced mare I believe you might enjoy." He didn't mention the lengths to which he'd gone to procure that particular mount some months prior. "We could have the kitchens prepare a basket of luncheon, for the seashore."

"I should enjoy that," Cecelia agreed readily, relieved at having what she expected to be a very strained evening turning out quite pleasant. "I do enjoy the sea."

"Somersett is on the shore also, is it not?" Julian was encouraged to find her relaxing with him.

"Yes, though but on a firth. We've only rock, not beach as Stanford has." Cecelia easily lapsed into telling Julian about her estate. "Somersett lies rather low. In fact, I engaged that young gentleman, Mr. Melville, to offer solutions to my drainage problems."

"That is what you were so engrossed in speaking to the man about at the viscountess's party?"

"Yes." Cecelia hesitated at something in the duke's tone. "Do you not think Melville is knowledgeable?"

Julian smiled, absurdly pleased that she should ask his opinion.

"Yes, he is quite. You made a wise decision. In fact, I had actually gone to the viscount's dinner just to meet Melville, and discuss that very subject with him. I had been under the impression we were but dining *en famille*."

Cecelia grinned in sudden understanding. "So you did not know the ladies of the household had two eligible daughters?"

The duke gave her a look. "Had I known that, I assure you, they would have seen naught but my regrets!"

Cecelia giggled. "But surely you enjoyed the girls' singing. I thought the little brunette had a rather enchanting voice."

"Not near so enchanting as some," the duke murmured but quickly moved to safer subjects at Cecelia's blush.

"But as to young Melville, he is scheduled to come to Stanford next week to check some marshland in the estate's western quarter. Perhaps you might wish to ride out with us in case the problems at Somersett are similar in nature?"

"Are you serious?" Cecelia looked up in surprise.

"Of course, unless you would prefer not."

"No, I would be most pleased to accompany you. I was just rather taken by surprise that you should ask."

"Oh?"

"Most men, or at least most that I've known, seldom consider a female capable of any degree of reasoning in business matters."

"Hopefully, I may be seen to judge a person on their merits rather than their gender," the duke declared a bit stiffly. At Cecelia's grin, he frowned.

"I said something amusing?"

"I am sorry. I could not help but recall how, despite Percival's assurances on my ability, that you insisted on your steward delivering and disbursing the payroll for *Justine.* I admit to a definite feeling that you did not think a female able to handle such funds."

Julian chuckled, rising to escort them from the dining room. "I fear, you have me. But my dear, I beg you recall that female was *not* the knowledgeable Baroness of her own Estate, but rather a delightful bit of muslin called Amber."

Cecelia accepted the duke's arm, though her smile had vanished at Julian's reminder of her indiscretion. "Of course. I suppose I could scarcely expect you to trust such a person."

The duke had not intended his teasing to be taken as chastisement. "Had I not been so blind, I should have." Julian turned her to him on entering back into the hall. "Cecelia, though I am yet appalled at the danger you put yourself into, I can only admire your courage and determination to help Percival. I hoped I had made it plain in my first letter that I held you in no less esteem despite that matter."

"You said that in the letter?"

Julian raised a brow, "I thought my letters were rather clear?"

"Oh," realizing belatedly what she had admitted, Cecelia stammered, "actually, they were not."

The duke frowned in remembered ire that she should have so patently ignored his avowals. "They were not? As I cannot imagine the words being simpler, perhaps it was my penmanship you had difficulty with?" he asked dryly.

Cecelia grimaced. "No, or at least not through your fault. The first two letters remained in Constance's father's coat pocket for well over two months," she finally admitted. "During their sojourn in his jacket, Mr. Talley was also caught in a rainstorm. I received your letters but some three weeks ago, when the Talleys arrived back from Scotland." Cecelia hesitated. "I fear I could read little of your first two communications as the ink had quite run from their soaking."

"What?" The duke glared down at Cecelia in frustration. "Why in the blue blazes did you not *tell* me you had not been able to read the letters?"

Cecelia's lips tightened. "After your third, and I might add, discouragingly curt communication, sir, it took me days to even dare the apology I managed."

"Damn it, Cecelia, do you realize—"

"Julian," Cecelia interrupted angrily. "I have no intention of standing here having you curse at me for something I had no control over! Now, perhaps you will excuse me."

Ayers, who had stayed discreetly from sight during the ensuing argument, cautiously entered the hallway. "Your Grace, shall you be wishing your port in your quarters tonight?"

"I suppose," Julian's countenance tightened grimly, "but make it scotch!"

* * *

Hannah turned when her mistress entered the room. "The housekeeper is seeing to bringing up a bath, my lady, shall I—" she stopped in concern at Cecelia's expression. "Oh, dear. Now what has happened?"

"Hannah, the man is absolutely impossible!" Cecelia flung herself onto the settee. "We were actually getting along quite well and then he—he—oh, it is useless," she sighed in distress. "It is quite apparent the duke simply does not care for me!"

"Now—" Hannah tried but Cecelia cut her off.

"No, there is no help for it, Hannah. Why he almost as much as implied downstairs that he liked Amber better! 'A delightful bit of muslin' he called her!"

Fortunately, Cecelia did not hear her maid's muttered, "Small wonder!"

"We've brought your hip tub, Your Grace." The housekeeper gestured a sturdy manservant to roll in the unwieldy device. "Put it by the fire there, Robert, and you may begin fetching the hot water. His Grace had hoped to have the new bathing room finished before your arrival, my lady," she chattered happily to Cecelia while laying out thick towels. "He plans to have that small dressing room between your quarters converted so that you should not have to have tubs brought up, but I suppose he has not been able to get the builders as of yet."

Cecelia looked at the housekeeper as though she'd lost her mind. "I imagine that would have been quite difficult to manage in but a day!"

"A day?" The woman looked at her in confusion, and then laughed. "Oh, Your Grace, you thought I meant he'd planned that since you two moved up the wedding date? Oh no, His Grace began months ago,

redecorating for you—I expect as soon as he asked you
to marry him! Why, the man was so anxious to be sure
you liked it here that we thought he was going to turn
the whole place upside down! But it was all so romantic!
If you'll forgive me, Your Grace," she rattled on comfortably not even noticing Cecelia's shocked silence, "it was
plain as a pikestaff to us all how much His Grace loved
you! Why would you believe, he himself actually went
through the linen drapers samples to choose the colors
for your rooms here. He drove that poor man quite to
distraction insisting he find this particular shade of deep
rose! Said it was something about a gown you had worn
when he first met you! He even hunted everywhere for
these thorny little bushes of *elegante* roses—because you
favored them. Half the greenhouse is now growing
them." She glanced over to the tub.

"That's fine, lads. We'll leave you to your bath now,
Your Grace." She bustled the waterboys out, slipping
some scented bath salts onto the table with a conspirato-
rial grin at Hannah. "Just ring if you need anything—
anything at all."

"Well, now, my lady, do you *still* believe the duke
cares naught for you?" Hannah inquired archly of Cecelia, once the housekeeper left.

Cecelia was looking about the lovely room in near
shock. "She said Julian did all this for me!"

"Months ago," Hannah added dryly.

"Oh Hannah, have I truly been such a blind fool?"
Cecelia moaned, wisely not waiting for an answer. "Do
you know what this means? Those letters—he must have
stated his intentions in those letters! No wonder he was
so upset about them! Oh, Hannah, what am I to do?"

"I should think it obvious, but first take your bath
before it gets cold," her maid directed quite unsympa-

thetically, unhooking her mistress's gown. "Now let me
pin your hair up before you get in the tub."

"What did you mean, it is obvious, what I should do?"
Cecelia leaned forward for the abigail to wash her back.
"Julian was truly so angry I don't think—"

"I'm sure His Grace will accept your apology, if you
just explain."

"Well, I will, of course apologize, assuming he ever
speaks to me again, though I don't know if he will."

"No, my lady. That is not at all what I meant," Hannah
said firmly. "This is your wedding night. If you wish to
save this marriage, you must not let your husband spend
it alone, brooding about some silly misunderstanding."

"Hannah, you are not suggesting—" Cecelia spun
her head to look at her abigail in shock. "I could never!
I cannot believe you would expect me to—I mean—"

"My lady, you *are* married. And, you must admit,
it is quite your own doing that has caused this whole
situation."

"Oh dear. No, I could never." Blushing, Cecelia
shook her head, dislodging further the pins holding
her hair up.

"Now, my lady, see what you've done!" Hannah
admonished in exasperation when Cecelia's heavy locks
slipped loose from their pins. "Your hair is quite
soaked!"

"It doesn't matter. No one shall see it."

Hannah tsked, continuing their argument. "And
what may I ask was so horrid about my suggestion? You
now know the man loves you. You don't want to lose
him do you?"

"No, of course I don't. And I do love him too, but I
just couldn't go to Julian. Hannah, what you suggest is
dreadfully improper! You don't understand. With nobil-

ity, it is the gentleman that should—well, it is just impossible for a *lady* to make such a move!''

"So, it is improper for a *lady* to approach a gentleman?''

"Yes, it just is not done.''

"Well, if you say so." Cecelia could not see her abigail's wry smile. "Now that you have gotten all of your hair wet, I suppose I may as well shampoo it. Here, my lady, why don't you just lean back here and close your eyes. Relax a bit, while I run get my shampoo. I'm sure you've probably given yourself a headache with all this tension.''

"Oh thank you, Hannah. That does feel much better," Cecelia sighed leaning back.

On returning Hannah carefully moved the hand mirror from the tub side table before filling the basin with warm water and the contents of the bottle she'd gone to fetch.

Cecelia managed to relax almost to the point of sleepiness while her abigail gently massaged her scalp.

"There now, my lady." Hannah considered her handiwork in pleasure, toweling the excess water from Cecelia's hair. "Now we'd best get you out of that tub before you get chilled. Here slip on this robe, and lie down on the settee by the fire so I may finish drying your hair.''

Cecelia did quite doze off for some minutes under Hannah's gentle ministrations of toweling and brushing her hair. When she awoke it was in surprise to find her abigail quite happily applying the curling iron.

"Hannah, whatever are you doing?" Cecelia sat up. "All that is not necessary when I am just going to go to bed." She caught sight of herself in the mirror over the mantel and gasped. "Oh my heavens! You dyed my hair!"

"Yes, my lady," her abigail answered, calmly picking up her styling apparatuses, "and curled it too."

Her mistress spun on her in fury but Hannah merely stepped safely back. "Now my lady, did you yourself not just tell me how you love the duke and do not wish to lose him?"

"What on earth does that have to—"

"Here missy." Hannah handed her mistress the mirror. "I think you are a lovelier Amber than you have ever been!"

"Amber?" Cecelia stopped and turned to the mirror. "Good heavens! You've turned me back into Amber." She was too amazed to even be angry.

"Well, you did say no *lady* could go to a gentleman? But if you'll recall, Amber was no lady." She smiled watching the slow grin touch her mistress's lips.

"Oh Hannah, I couldn't."

"No?"

"I simply could never." The very outrageousness of the idea however dissolved Cecelia's anger and she chuckled, turning the mirror to consider the cascades of red hair falling down her back.

"Of course, the new duchess couldn't!" Hannah agreed staunchly. "The duchess is a *lady*, but Amber could." She held out a lacy rose peignoir enticingly.

"Oh, my word. Wherever did you get that?" Cecelia stared at the night dress in amazement.

"I found it, hanging in that armoire, when I put up your clothes." Hannah grinned. "His Grace has apparently been quite thorough."

"Are you serious? Julian had purchased that for *me*?"

"I should scarcely think he intended it for Mrs. Bond."

Cecelia giggled, and unable to resist, slipped out of her robe and let the silken garment slide over her head.

"Oh my, oh my!" she gasped on turning back to the mirror.

"Oh my, indeed!" Hannah sighed. "I am certain you need have no fears of His Grace remaining angry at you in *that!*"

"Hannah, I-I really cannot," Cecelia laughed shakily, yet looking at her image. "I know you do mean well but can you imagine how embarrassing if I just—oh no, I can't."

"Now, Miss Cecelia, you got rave reviews for your acting in *Justine*. In fact, that night Mr. Levison took me to the theater, I myself saw you dancing about with that good looking actor man, all hugged up. Why, I do believe at one point you actually kissed him, did you not?"

"That was only a stage kiss," Cecelia objected. "And, if you're suggesting that I act—"

"What I'm suggesting is just that you again become Amber. It didn't seem to bother you to cuddle up to that actor as her—"

"You are right, it really didn't bother me at all," Cecelia said thoughtfully.

"Of course it didn't. You were being Justine. And as Amber, I recall at least one occasion by that stream, that you weren't over reticent at *playing* the part of the duke's mistress? In fact, I could almost avow you were enjoying it."

Cecelia was too caught up in the possibilities to really give much time to chastising her impudent maid. "Do you really think I dare? Oh no, I could not—but—"

Hannah remained carefully silent.

Cecelia turned yet again to the mirror and lifted her mass of curls tentatively. "I don't suppose you have a rose colored ribbon?"

* * *

The duke sat before the fire in his quarters quite morosely staring at the boring government treatise he hoped might eventually put him to sleep.

Unable to concentrate on the pages, he found his mind once again wandering to the woman in the next room and grimaced in chagrin. He had had no right to round on Cecelia so over those letters.

It was just that it had caused him such accursed distress to imagine she had cared so little for his declaration of love as to ignore it! And *then,* to find she had been unable to even read the blamed letters!

Julian scowled. To think that *his* letters had remained in some fool farmer's coat pocket for over two months! The duke allowed himself a few moments of pleasingly murderous thoughts toward Percival's bucolic relation.

Why in heaven's name could Cecelia not have simply told him what happened to the letters from the start? Women were so bloody difficult! No, Julian corrected his thoughts, it was not *all* women who were difficult, only ladies!

He had always managed to get along quite well with his various mistresses. Even with Amber, or Cecelia when she was Amber—Julian smiled to himself in fond remembrance. Indeed, the little minx had quite enchanted him! The duke sighed deeply, staring into the glowing embers of his fire. He almost wished his Amber had truly been naught but what she seemed and could be here tonight with him in his arms.

The duke barely heard the slight tap on the door and glanced over to the hall entrance irritably. He had told Ayers he would need nothing else that evening. "Yes, what is it?"

The duke stood up in surprise when, not the hall

door as he'd expected, but the one behind him to the connecting chamber opened.

Julian stared speechless as the vision of his recent thoughts seemed magically to manifest herself before him. He had to be dreaming.

"Cecelia?" the duke finally managed hoarsely.

"Cecelia?" the woman laughed lightly. *"Au contraire, monsieur,* it is I, Amber."

The duke stood quite incapable of movement as the auburn-haired minx glided toward him. "I fear, Your Grace, that silly new duchess of yours was much too proud to come and apologize to you tonight, so . . ."

A slow smile of understanding moved the duke's lips when she stepped up and shyly adjusted the lapels of his robe. "So I thought that I should come and see if perhaps there was anything I might do to help matters?"

Julian chuckled, allowing his eyes to roam appreciatively over his mistress.

"Why yes, my love," he murmured drawing his delightful bride to him. "I do expect I might be able to think of—something."

The duke's lips silenced his duchess's most unseemly giggle.

FROM AWARD-WINNING AUTHOR
JO BEVERLEY